WILFRED
THE (UN) WISE

WILFRED

THE (UN) WISE

Cas Lester

Illustrated by
Mark Beech

Piccadilly
PRESS

First published in Great Britain in 2016 by
PICCADILLY PRESS
80–81 Wimpole St, London W1G 9RE
www.piccadillypress.co.uk

A CIP catalogue record for this book is available from the British Library.

ISBN: 978-1-8481-2464-6
also available as an ebook

Typeset in Sabon 11/16 pt by
Palimpsest Book Production Limited, Falkirk, Stirlingshire
Printed and bound by Clays Ltd, St Ives Plc

Piccadilly Press is an imprint of Bonnier Publishing Fiction,
a Bonnier Publishing company
www.bonnierpublishingfiction.co.uk
www.bonnierpublishing.co.uk

For the Drs Bratt
with apologies
thanks
and
love

Chapter One

Wilfred the Wise

Whistling horribly tunelessly, Wilfred carelessly slung his Bag of Bees magik charm on its tatty bit of string around his impressively grubby neck. You would have thought he'd take more care of it (the charm, I mean, not his neck) since it was meant to be his most prized possession. Not to mention his only possession. (Well, apart from the tatty brown tunic and leggings he stood up in, and his scruffy leather boots.)

But to be honest, Wilfred (or 'Wilfred the Wise' as he preferred to be called) was disappointed with the charm. It didn't seem to give him much magik power and he wasn't even convinced there were any bees inside. He'd never heard them buzzing. Maybe they were dead? He didn't dare open the bag and check, worried that the magik might fall out and he'd get into dire trouble with the wizard. So he'd decided not to mention it, and not to worry about it either.

Which *was* wise, because the aforementioned wizard was none other than Wincewart the Withering, Castle Mage, Soothsaying Sage and the greatest wizard in all Wallop in the Wold. And poor Wilfred was his apprentice.

Wincewart had given Wilfred the charm as soon as he was old enough to start learning magik, and at first he'd worn it proudly. It had shown everyone he wasn't merely a peasant boy, but a wizard's apprentice. But now the bag was shabby and grimy, and showed everyone he was *still* only an apprentice, with only a novice's charm – not a fully fledged wizard with a proper talisman of potency.

Poor Wilfred felt like he'd been an apprentice for *ever*. He didn't know how many years he'd spent living in the gloomy hermit cave tucked under the hill. But then he had no idea how old he was either – somewhere between being old enough to start learning magik, and too young to shave.

But he did know that at the rate Wincewart was teaching him, he was going to stay an apprentice for ever *and a day* and would never become famous as 'Wilfred the Wise', the youngest wizard in all Wallop in the Wold. That was his dream – nay, his destiny.

Or so he hoped.

Ye simple, easy basic magik

The problem was, Wincewart would only let him study the most simple, easy, basic magik. And he made him repeat it over and over, until Wilfred could do it perfectly. So Wilfred, understandably, got bored and sloppy and made mistakes, and the elderly wizard would raise a withering eyebrow, sigh dramatically, and make him start again.

All this month, to Wilfred's frustration, Wincewart had ordered him to master the most ridiculously simple spells for lighting and snuffing candles. So Wilfred had dutifully practised Ye Simple Lighting

Spell (well, a bit) and had actually managed to get a candle to light a couple of times. But he couldn't see the point of learning Ye Simple Snuffing Spell (which was just doing Ye Simple Lighting Spell in reverse). It was tricky to learn the incantation backwards, and anyway, why bother when you could just blow the candle out?

Wilfred itched to do something more impressive.

So secretly he had 'borrowed' Wincewart's spell book (*Ye Ancient Complete Runic Record of Magik Charms and Enchantments*) and flicked through the pages to find a more ambitious spell to teach himself.

He'd chosen Ye Spectacular Summoning Charm. It was a complicated piece of high magik, but Wilfred 'the Wise' was convinced he could master it – and then he would show Wincewart what he was really capable of.

As it turned out, it was a very *unwise* thing to do.

Ye Spectacular Summoning Charm

Wilfred had actually practised Ye Spectacular Summoning Charm quite a bit And, to be fair to him, he'd more or less got the hang of it. (Although I should probably stress the word 'less'.) So he'd pleaded with Wincewart to let him perform it in front of him, and finally the elderly wizard (pestered to within an inch of the end of this tether) had unwisely given in.

Bright and early the following morning, Wilfred had gathered together the magikal items for the enchantment, slung his Bag of Bees charm around his neck, and prepared to dazzle his master with his astounding talents.

Wincewart the Withering sat in his ornately carved wooden chair at the head of the huge oak table. His long white hair and even longer white beard spilled down over his wizarding robe, and he gazed sternly out from under his grizzled eyebrows at the scruffy boy before him in the middle of the cave.

There was a sudden fluttering of wings as a large bird landed on his shoulder. It was Bertram the Beady, a magnificent jet-black raven with sharp eyes, a sharper beak and even sharper tongue. 'Bertram the Bossy' was probably a better name for the bird. But then the raven was the wizard's invaluable familiar – a fact that went to his head, or rather to his beak. Wincewart took Bertram everywhere. He was convinced the bird gave him good luck, added status and, more importantly, a little bit more power.

Eleventh century sorcery was a competitive business, and frankly Wincewart needed all the extra potency he could get. (Truth be told, the wizard was nowhere near as powerful as he claimed to be.)

Right now, Wilfred didn't know which of them was making him more nervous – the elderly wizard or his arrogant familiar. But he took a deep breath, plucked up his courage, and began: 'I art Wilfred the Wise –' he announced confidently.

But he was rudely interrupted by a raucous screech of laughter from Bertram. 'Wilfred the *Wise*!' he crowed. 'The *Wise*? Who art thou kidding?'

Doing his best to ignore the interruption, Wilfred continued.

'Master, thou will be astonished by the magik I will perform for thee.'

Bertram and Wincewart exchanged looks. Bertram's was sceptical; Wincewart's was downright anxious.

With a great flourish, Wilfred took up a piece of

chalk and drew a large six-pointed star on the rough stone floor. Which was a shame, because it was meant to be a pentacle. He looked at it doubtfully. It didn't look right. So he counted the points and hurriedly rubbed it out and (correctly) drew a five-pointed star instead. Wincewart groaned witheringly.

Undeterred, Wilfred picked up a purple spell candle and lit it from one of the wall torches that burned day and night in the dim cave. (Well, it was much easier than using Ye Simple Lighting Spell – a fact that did not escape the notice of his master, who rolled his eyes in despair.)

Then, stepping inside the pentacle, and clutching his Bag of Bees, Wilfred boldly declared, 'To thy amazement I shall perform Ye Spectacular Summoning Charm!' He paused, hoping for an impressed reaction from the wizard. He didn't get one, so he carried on.

'Thy silver dragon's claw talisman will unpin itself from thy robe, and fly into mine hand.'

Wincewart's valuable, solid silver talisman of potency was the elderly wizard's most treasured possession. He never took it off. It stayed pinned on his robe, next to his second-most treasured possession: his three-foot-long white beard. What

Wilfred was proposing was as audacious as it was ambitious.

Bertram cawed in disbelief.

Wincewart raised one bushy eyebrow. 'Art thou sure thou can do this?' he said.

'Trust me, I be a wizard!' grinned Wilfred.

'Huh!' scoffed Bertram. 'Thou be a wizard's apprentice, and a very poor one at that!'

Ignoring Bertram's dig, Wilfred confidently (theatrically, even) uttered the magikal enchantment. Tragically, under Wincewart's stern gaze, he got flustered and muddled the words.

There was a violent flash of turquoise-coloured lightning, and a shower of hot red sparks and,

WHOOOSH! WHUMPH!

Wincewart's beloved white beard burst into flames.

Chapter Two

Wilfred's worst catastrophe (so far)

'Witches' warts!' roared the wizard. 'I'm on fire!'

Flames shot up from his magnificent long, white beard, scorching his bushy eyebrows and burning the tip of his nose.

WHOOSH! FRIZZLE . . . FIZZ . . . !

Squawking hysterically, Bertram flapped off Wincewart's shoulder, his large wings fanning the fire and making it worse.

'Boars' buttocks!' gasped Wilfred, and he desperately looked around the cave for the bucket, intending to throw its contents over the flames. Which, when you stop to think what the bucket was usually used for in a cave without a toilet, wouldn't have exactly helped endear him to his master.

Fortunately there was no need for the bucket because Wincewart had hurriedly conjured up a short, sharp, indoor rain shower, and extinguished the blaze.

SIZZLE . . .

HISSSSS . . .

There was a horrible silence – and an even more horrible smell.

With the remains of his treasured beard now charred and steaming, Wincewart slowly turned to fix his furious gaze on his young apprentice.

'Dragons' teeth, boy!' he growled. 'Thou art as much use as a cracked cauldron!'

Wilfred gulped and pushed his fingers nervously through his scruffy hair. 'Master, I did not mean to set thee on fire! I truly thought I could do the spell.

Will thou forgive me?' he begged humbly and, frankly, ridiculously optimistically.

Wilfred was a hopeless apprentice. He'd had countless accidents, and caused no end of chaos. But looking on the bright side (as Wilfred usually did) he had treated Wincewart to some spectacularly entertaining disasters, not to mention the occasional explosion.

Once, when he'd been grinding ingredients together, he'd muddled toadflax with fleabane. The mixture had seethed and bubbled, then erupted like a volcano and they'd both had to clamber on top of the table for safety. (Which, let's face it, wasn't a very elegant position for an elderly wizard.)

Another time, brewing a bewitching potion, Wilfred had carelessly added ten times the amount of powdered unicorn horn needed for the spell. The cauldron had exploded – spectacularly. Wilfred had ducked but Wincewart had been splattered from the top of his pointed hat to the hem of his long robe, and had come out in a nasty rash of boils.

But setting fire to Wincewart's beloved three-foot-long pristine white beard was Wilfred's worst catastrophe ever. (Well, so far.)

Bertram the Beady opens his big beak

'Did I not tell thee the boy was a dolt?' crowed Bertram. 'And that thou would be better off with a hedgehog as an apprentice? And a dead and roasted one at that?'

Wincewart nodded his white-haired head gravely. 'Thou did.'

'And did thou listen? Thou did not!' gloated his familiar. 'I know not why thou let him call himself Wilfred the Wise! He should be called Wilfred the Unwise!'

Wilfred hung his head. He had wanted to impress his master so much, but had failed so dramatically – and so often.

Suddenly, the elderly wizard clutched at his chest, gasped and reeled backwards. 'My talisman!' he cried. 'It has gone!'

Unseen by Wincewart, and defying all of the ancient wizard's expectations, the silver talisman had obediently followed Wilfred's command, unpinned itself, and shot off across the cave. And amidst all the confusion of the smoke and the flames and the burning beard, no one had seen it go – or where it had landed.

'What has thou done with it?' roared Wincewart.

Panic washed over Wilfred's grimy face. (Which was more than a soapy flannel had ever done.) Shoving his mop of brown hair out of his eyes, he looked frantically around the hermit cave. There was no sign of the talisman and he hadn't the faintest idea where it could be.

'Frogs' farts! I know not, master!' he cried. 'I be sorry!'

'Sorry? Thou *will* be sorry, thou lumpen, maggot-ridden turnip-headed idiot!' raged the wizard.

'Bertram, can thou not see it anywhere with thy beady eyes?' Wilfred pleaded.

Bertram could not.

'Can thou not undo the magik and get thy talisman back, master?' asked Wilfred hopefully.

Up until now, Wincewart had always managed to undo the disasters his over-ambitious apprentice had caused, simply by reversing the magik.

'No, I cannot this time,' he snapped. 'If thou had done the spell correctly, then I could. But thou muttered and muddled and I have no idea exactly what thou said! Do thou?' he demanded.

Sheepishly, Wilfred had to admit he did not.

'Then I cannot utter what thou said backwards,

15

can I?' spluttered Wincewart. 'How often must I tell thee not to mess with magik thou does not understand?'

Wilfred bit his lip and said nothing.

Bertram the Beady put his head on one side. 'Thou art in big trouble now, Wilfred the Unwise,' he squawked.

Wilfred shot the bird a dirty look.

Too much magikal kit and caboodle

'Hags' curses!' swore Wincewart and then, looking at the hour candle, which was slowly but surely burning down on the large oak table, he turned to Bertram and added, 'We must go to the castle. Lord Wallop wishes to speak with me about the Midsummer Merrymaking of Magik and Mages. And that clot-head has already made us late.' He grabbed his wizard's staff and glared at Wilfred. 'Thou will stay here and find my talisman, and thou will *not* leave the cave until thou has done so!'

Wincewart turned on his heel, wrapped his cloak tightly round him to hide the charred remains of his beard, and stormed out.

Bertram, wobbling ridiculously on Wincewart's

shoulder, screeched back at Wilfred: 'And thou can clean up my droppings, chop the kindling and keep the fire burning. We do not want a cave full of wolves or dragons . . .'

His voice faded away.

'Cuckoos' spit and chickens' snot!' swore Wilfred, sitting down heavily on the wizard's massive oak chair. Kicking his legs idly, he stared enviously at the bright sunny day. Wincewart hardly ever took him up to the castle, but Bertram the Beady got to go *everywhere* with him. It wasn't fair. *And* he was missing out on the excitement of getting ready for the Midsummer Merrymaking of Magik and Mages, *and* stuck in a gloomy hermit cave with only spiders and maybugs for company. He bet the other village lads would be up at the castle, helping or larking around having a good time. But if he wanted to join them, he'd have to find the talisman.

'Hey ho. It will not find itself,' he told himself. So, whistling cheerfully (and horribly out of tune), he got up to look for it.

Wincewart had a great quantity of magikal kit and caboodle – not to mention countless magikal charms and other paraphernalia of potency (like I said – he needed all the extra power he could get)

– so hunting through it all took Wilfred ages.

He peered into the cauldrons and rummaged through the enormous wooden chest, which was crammed with star charts, quill pens, ink and coloured spell candles. He quickly rootled around the table between some weighing scales and the huge pestle and mortar he used for grinding spell ingredients together. And he almost knocked Wincewart's scrying glass to the floor, only just catching the crystal orb as it rolled off the edge of the table.

He had a quick look through the jars of potions, oils and herbs, and the boxes of crystals, charm stones, amulets and spell bones. But he still couldn't find the talisman and pretty soon he was bored.

Outside the dim cave a steady stream of people was heading up the hill to the castle in the bright sunshine. Their laughter drifted across the hillside and into the cave.

Wilfred longed to go too, but he didn't dare disobey Wincewart. He'd never forget when his master had given him the ears of a donkey, the feet of a chicken, and the tail of a pig – just for being cheeky.

So he looked all around the floor and under the table, and even shook out the sheepskins on Wincewart's bed. As he did so, a cloud of dust billowed into his face. Coughing and spluttering, he went over to the pantry shelf and took a swift glug of ale from the jug to clear his throat. Then he poked around between the remains of a dry loaf, two wrinkled mangel-wurzels and some limp nettles. But the silver dragon's claw talisman wasn't anywhere to be seen.

'Maybug belches,' he sighed. 'I give up.'

Do not call me Wincewart!

'By the bewitching bones of Blodwin the Bold, that boy will be the death of me!' raged Wincewart as he strode up the hill towards the castle, his dark blue cloak billowing around him melodramatically. He thumped his wizard's staff heavily onto the ground as he spoke. 'He does not work (*thump*), he does not listen (*thump*), he does not learn (*thump*), he does not try (*thump*). He does drive me to madness!'

'I know not why thou keeps him, Wincewart,' squawked Bertram from his shoulder. It was a bumpy way to travel, but it was easier on the wings.

The wizard stopped dead in his tracks, and the startled bird fell off his shoulder. 'Do not call me

Wincewart!' he snapped. 'Do I need to remind thee that I be Wincewart the Withering, Castle Mage, Soothsaying Sage and the greatest wizard in all Wallop in the Wold?'

'Thou art the *only* wizard in all Wallop in the Wold!' squawked Bertram dryly.

Wincewart harrumphed crossly. 'How many times must I tell thee? Thou must call me master.'

Bertram fluttered his wings indignantly. 'But thou art not my master! A familiar to a wizard be like a stick to an old man. Thou art an old man and thou cannot walk without thy stick.'

'I be a wizard, not an old man! And this be a staff, not a stick,' thundered Wincewart, waving his staff threateningly. 'And thou can call me "O formidable one", or "O mighty wizard" or "my sage" or . . .'

'"My sage"?' cawed Bertram gleefully. 'Like the herb? Why not "my parsley" or "my lemon mint"?'

'No! Not sage like the herb! Sage, meaning someone wise, clever and knowing,' snapped Wincewart.

He stomped on in an increasingly flaming temper, with Bertram fluttering after him, wisely keeping out of range of the wizard's long staff.

Chapter Three

Ye Olde Yet Effective Runic Foretelling Spell

Wilfred sprawled in his master's chair with his leg draped over one arm, daydreaming. In his mind's eye, he, Wilfred the Wise, was astounding crowds of people at the castle with a dazzling display of magic. He'd enchanted a piglet to sing, turned a pewter cup into a gold chalice, and for the big finish, conjured up a fire-breathing dragon! The applause was deafening and Wincewart declared himself astonished.

But Wilfred came suddenly down to earth, realising he was stuck in the hermit cave and not even allowed to go to the castle. But, oddly, he cheered up when he recalled Bertram's squawked instructions. Because doing chores meant *doing magik*.

So he cheerfully muttered Ye Basic Sweeping Enchantment to command the hazel broom to clean up Bertram's bird poo, and Ye Basic Chopping Charm to make the axe cut kindling. Then, happily ducking the resulting shower of sparks, he flung more wood onto the fire (which he'd forgotten to keep an eye on) and, after a few failed attempts at Ye Simple Lighting Spell, got it going again. A thin pall of turquoise smoke drifted round the cave from all the sparks and magik.

Of course, this might sound impressive nowadays, but actually these were spells that any novice apprentice could do. (And usually without creating such an embarrassing amount of sparks and smoke.)

But nevertheless, Wilfred sat at the head of the huge oak table highly pleased with himself. 'I have fine wizarding skills, and one day, I *will* be a mighty magician.'

In his heart, Wilfred knew he was a poor apprentice. But that didn't stop him dreaming. Not because he wanted power and status (well, it was *partly* that) but because he wanted to make Wincewart proud of him. Odd though it might seem, and even though the wizard was easily old enough to be his great-great grandfather, Wincewart was the nearest thing to family Wilfred had.

No one knew who Wilfred's parents were, nor why he had been dumped outside the castle walls when he was a very small boy, with nothing except the clothes he stood up in, an honest face, a cheery outlook and a lopsided sheepish grin to help him make his way in the world. Wincewart had stumbled upon him (fortunately not literally) on his way home one night. Since the mighty gates were shut and all the guards were in bed, he decided to take the small boy in – just for the night . . .

But by the morning, the aforementioned honest face, cheery outlook and lopsided sheepish grin had worked their magik on the elderly wizard, and Wincewart decided to raise the boy as his own. He called him Wilfred and determined to teach him everything he knew. A task that was proving far harder than anyone could have thought possible.

But anyhow, now that Wilfred had finished his chores he was stuck in the cave, bored to death. A large, red leather-bound book lay on the table near his elbow. It was Wincewart's grimoire: his master's valuable, actually make that *invaluable*, book of spells: *Ye Ancient Yet Complete Runic Record of Magik Charms and Enchantments.*

An idea flickered like a pale candle flame in his mind. Wincewart would be gone for hours yet so he'd have plenty of time . . . plenty of time to try to do a foretelling enchantment to see if, one day, he would indeed become a great wizard! (And I stress the word, 'try'.)

Excited, Wilfred flicked through the enormous grimoire. He was baffled by most of the magik symbols, but he could read the rest of the text (well, some of it – he struggled with the bit written in runes).

He wisely chose the simplest predicting enchantment he could find:

Ye Olde Yet Effective Runic Foretelling Spell
Thou needest:
a scrying glass
a purple spell candle
one dragon's scale
chalk

Thou must:
Draw a pentacle upon ye ground. Light ye spell candle and place it in ye centre, with ye dragon's scale. Then take up thy scrying glass and step inside ye magik pentacle, gaze into ye depths of thy glass and utter ye ancient enchantment:

ᚠᛋ · ᛁ · ᚲᚠᛋᛏᛝᚦ · ᚦᛁᛋ · ᛋᚲᛗᛚᛚ ⁚

ᚦ ᛗ · ᚤᚾᛏᚢᚱᛗ · ᚤᚠᚱᛗᛏᛗᛚᛚ

(Which, in case you're a bit rusty at reading runes, says:
As I cast this spell
Ye future foretell.)

It seemed simple enough. With mounting excitement Wilfred gathered together everything he'd need. Lastly, with trembling hands, he took Wincewart's scrying glass out of its wooden case.

On the spur of the moment, he pulled on Wincewart's best wizarding cloak – the midnight-blue one covered in magikal symbols stitched in gold. The long, flowing robe made him feel like a powerful wizard. Sadly, since it was several sizes too big, it made him *look* ridiculous. But it's the thought that counts.

Cradling the scrying glass in his grubby hands, he stepped into the pentacle and recited the words of the enchantment (well, very nearly). Then, as the crystal ball flooded with swirls of inky blue, just to make sure it was clear what he wanted, Wilfred added, 'Show me the future!' in a commanding voice.

There was a flash of brilliant white light, a puff of turquoise smoke and:

KABOOM!

The spell candle was blown out, the scrying glass fell from his hands, and Wilfred the Wise disappeared.

Chapter Four

B-Dazzle

WITHERING WALLOP IN THE WOLD – NOWADAYS

Just after 7.15 a.m., about a thousand years later, Bel was in her PJs, on her knees, digging around in her wardrobe for the *perfect* outfit. (Nothing odd in that, maybe, except that it was the summer holidays so she didn't have to be up anywhere *near* that early, and normally she wasn't interested in clothes *at all.*)

Nevertheless, she busily hurled things over her

head and onto one of two piles behind her. Mentally she'd labelled the pile on the bed 'Maybe?' and the one on the floor 'NO WAY!'.

The 'NO WAY!' heap was way bigger than the 'Maybe?' – and growing rapidly.

'Nope!' she cried, ruthlessly flinging a flowery top onto the floor. 'Way too girly.' Then she chucked a red checked shirt after it. 'Definitely not!'

Pulling out a stripy top, she regarded it critically. 'Possible,' she said, dumping it on the bed.

'Nope, nope, nope!' (Two polo shirts and a pair of yellow shorts.)

'When did I get this? And WHY?' (Pink ra-ra skirt.)

'Too casual.' (Denim shorts.)

'Too *old*!' (White cardigan.)

'Nope, nope, noooooo!' (Everything else.)

Almost the entire contents of her wardrobe lay on the floor. There were only two items in the 'Maybe?' pile, so she ditched her PJs and tried them on: a pair of black leggings and a black-and-white striped top. Then she stood looking at herself in the long mirror she'd got her dad to stick on the wall.

'Not bad – but needs a certain something,' she judged.

Standing on tiptoes, she stretched up and took her black pork-pie hat off the top of the wardrobe, and tried cramming it onto her mass of dark curly hair. It was promising.

She was after a certain look; a statement. The kind of cool, bold style you'd need if you were going to be a famous street magician, with a string of drop-dead-brilliant illusions, a pile of videos on YouTube . . . *and* a seriously sassy name like B-Dazzle.

She struck a pose in front of the mirror, pretending she'd just finished astounding a crowd with a dazzling piece of magic, then looked her reflection straight in the eye and grinned.

'How did I do that?' she asked herself sassily. 'It's magic! I'm B-Dazzle and you've been B-Dazzled!'

She gave herself a cheeky wink.

'Oh yuk, NO! I hate the wink!' She cringed. 'Far too cheesy. The hat, on the other hand, is perfect. Positively B-dazzling!' Then, catching her eye in the mirror she said sternly, 'Hey – less playing with the hat and more rehearsing with the phone!'

But now her room looked more like the school's lost property dump than a rehearsal space. She couldn't practise in a messy room. It was unprofessional. So, scooping up armfuls of her clothing, she shoved it all back in the wardrobe and wedged the door closed.

The Incredible Phone Illusion

For weeks, Bel had been working up an ambitiously complicated trick involving a rucksack, two phones and a large cardboard box. When (or, I should probably say, 'if') she was ever confident enough to actually try it out in the street, it would eventually also include a bus stop and a queue of unsuspecting bystanders. (And when I say 'complicated' I mean I'm not even going to attempt to explain it here.)

She was trying to perfect the bit where she slid one of the phones up her sleeve, while picking up the large cardboard box at the same time. She'd managed it a few times but, being brutally honest with herself, if she looked closely in the mirror she could see the phone going up her sleeve. She needed to either get the sliding move slicker, or hide the action with the box – or both.

She tried again.

And again.

And again.

And again.

It was a knack. That was all there was to it, she told herself, and once you'd got the hang of it you just had to practise it until it was perfect *every single time.*

She'd just managed to neatly slip the phone up her sleeve with her thumb, and pick up the box with the rest of her hand, when the phone rang! She jumped, and it slid out of her sleeve and dropped on the floor.

She snatched up the phone and answered it. 'Hello?'

'Why have you got my phone?' asked a voice.

'I'm practising!'

'Well, practise with yours!'

'I am. But I need two phones for the trick, and anyway, Mum, how are you calling me if I've got your phone?'

'I'm on your dad's phone! Come down for breakfast and say goodbye to him. And bring my phone with you!'

Hurriedly Bel grabbed both phones, the rucksack, and the cardboard box and belted downstairs so fast she nearly tripped.

'Dad, wait!' she called. 'Can I show you something?'

About to be B-Dazzled

Bel's mum, Gloria, ran the Enchanted Cave Cafe, and they all lived in the flat above it. In the kitchen, her mum and dad were both dressed and ready for work, Mum in smart black trousers, a crisp white shirt and a black apron, and with her curly black hair tied up neatly. Bel's dad wore his tatty, old, *'Trust me, I'm a wizard!'* T-shirt, frayed jeans and sandals, his balding hair in a ponytail.

'Prepare to be B-Dazzled!' declared Bel, dumping the box on the kitchen worktop. She fiddled with the settings on both phones, put hers inside her rucksack, clipped it shut and slung the bag on her back. Then she slipped her mum's phone into her PJ pocket. 'OK, pretend you're just normal people . . .' began Bel.

'Oi! We *are* normal people!' laughed her dad.

Bel gave him a withering look. 'No, you're not. Trust me, you're *not* normal,' she said dryly, and her parents grinned. 'Anyways,' she continued, 'pretend you're a normal couple waiting for a bus.'

'What number bus?' asked her dad.

'Muuum – tell him!' protested Bel.

'Pack it in, Jon. Give her a chance,' said her mum, giving him a playful shove.

Bel picked up the cardboard box in both hands, but suddenly the phone in her pocket rang. 'Oh, that's my phone!' she cried, flustered. 'Can you just hold this while I answer it?' Hurriedly, she thrust the box at Jon, who instinctively took it. 'Sorry, sorry, thanks!' she blustered.

She fumbled to get the phone out of her pocket, but it had stopped ringing. 'Oh, I missed it,' she groaned, taking the box back from Jon – *and skillfully slipping the phone up her sleeve at the same time.*

Then she pretended to notice it was missing. 'Hey, where's my phone? I had it in my hand . . . it's just disappeared!'

Bel's performance was so convincing that her parents started to look for the phone. They assumed she must have dropped it on the floor. But within seconds, it rang again . . . and from *inside* her rucksack – which was still on her back, and still clipped shut!

She handed the box to her dad again, undid her rucksack and took out her phone!

'There it is!' she cried, giving them a broad grin.

'So, how did I do that?' she asked sassily. 'It's magic! I'm B-Dazzle and you've been B-Dazzled!' And she doffed her pork-pie hat at them and bowed.

'Hey, how cool was that?' cried Jon.

'Very impressive!' grinned Gloria. 'But seriously, where *is* my phone?'

With great panache and style, Bel slid her mum's phone out of her sleeve. 'Ta da!'

Jon plucked Bel's hat off her head and plonked a kiss on her hair. 'Awesome, dudette, simply awesome!' he announced. Then he shoved her hat back on her head, and headed off to work, pausing only to kiss Gloria as he swanned out.

Street magician – the clue's in the name

'Honestly, Mum, what did you think?' Bel asked anxiously, following Gloria through into the cafe, and helping herself to a cinnamon pastry.

'Well, apart from the fact that your phone is blue and mine is white, so it's obvious you used two phones . . . not bad!' grinned Gloria.

'Well, yeah, *and* the fact that your phone is snazzy and brand new, and my phone is tatty and *so* old it's practically from the Middle Ages!' agreed Bel. 'Which is why I need one like yours!'

'Hey, you're not conning me into buying you a new phone just so you can do a magic trick!'

'Mum, this is my career we're talking about! You'll regret it when I'm rich and famous!' she warned, grinning. 'Trust me, I'm a magician!'

'Nice try, kiddo, but no!'

The problem with having a businesswoman for a mum is that she's way too smart to be bamboozled, thought Bel.

Abandoning her new phone campaign, she said, 'Are you sure you didn't see the phone going up my sleeve?'

'Yes! I think the box was in the way.'

'Can I do it again, and this time you watch the phone?' begged Bel.

'Sorry, love, I haven't got time. I've got to open up and, anyhow, people aren't going to look that closely, believe me. People *want* to believe in magic. Why don't you practise on the customers in the cafe?'

'No chance!'

'Why not? It might magic up more business! Free Wi-Fi, free ketchup . . . and free show!'

Bel cringed. 'Mum, seriously, no!'

Bel refused point-blank to perform in front of strangers. She wouldn't even do the school talent contest. The only people she felt comfortable rehearsing in front of were Sara and Kelly, her best mates. But Sara's family had taken Kelly camping with them for two weeks, so until they were back, Bel was stuck with only her mum and dad to practise on.

The problem was, her parents never criticised – even if she dropped all her props, forgot her banter and did the trick back-to-front, inside-out and upside-down. Frankly, if she'd fallen flat on her face in a bowl of cold custard, they'd have applauded wildly and said she was brilliant.

Gloria unlocked the door to the cafe and Bel helped her set up tables and chairs on the pavement outside. Gloria gave her daughter a look.

'Listen, B-Dazzle, you can't do everything perfectly every time. If you want to succeed, then you have to let yourself fail sometimes.'

'I do!' protested Bel. 'Just not in public. I'd die! And it'd ruin my reputation.'

'Bel, you can't build a reputation as a street magician if you only perform in your bedroom!'

laughed her mum. 'The clue's in the name: *street* magician!'

Bel rolled her eyes.

Chapter Five

A thousand years is a long way to fall

In a side alley off the High Street, something – or rather *someone* – had just materialised in thin air. Fortunately nobody noticed, because *unfortunately* this someone had materialised *inside* the industrial-sized wheely bin belonging to the Enchanted Cave Cafe – and it hadn't been emptied for days. But, looking on the bright side, that did make it a soft place to land. Which was a good thing, because a thousand years is a long way to fall.

Wilfred the Wise lay sprawled in the dark and

smelly silence of the bin. 'Aaaaaaaargh!' he screamed. 'I have died!'

But then he thought, *Wait! If I have died, why can I talk? And why be it so smelly in here?* He struggled to his feet, his head pushing open the lid of the wheely bin.

'Joy be mine! I be not dead!' he cried, looking around him and brushing off the worst of the food and rubbish from his, or rather Wincewart's, cloak. 'Badgers' buttocks! What be this?' he cried, peeling a strange yellow and brown leathery thing off his tunic, and peering at it before dropping it onto the heap of rubbish under his feet.

Suddenly:

SWOOOSH!

There was a sound like rushing wind, and Wilfred saw a brightly coloured cart sweep past the end of the alley at incredible speed.

SWOOOSH!

There went another one. Wilfred hitched up Wincewart's cloak, leapt out of the bin, ran to get a better look and emerged in the middle of a small town.

Wilfred reeled. *What strange land be this?* More carts swept past in their brilliantly coloured tin armour. Then a man in a shiny black helmet rode by on a narrow two-wheeled barrow.

Wilfred looked around, fascinated. He was in a strange market place so big that a large lane ran down the middle. Metal lantern poles stood at either side, their coloured lights changing from red to orange to green and then back again.

Ravens' rumps! he thought, looking round to see who was doing Ye Basic Colour Changing Enchantment so well. But it was impossible to tell – there were so many witches and wizards milling around. In theory it was a simple enough spell, and even Wilfred could do it, but it tended to be quite noticeable when he did, with a lot of accidental sparks and smoke.

'Sheep snot and dragons' droppings!'

Boldly Wilfred stepped into the street. No one batted an eyelid at the sight of a young boy wandering around in a midnight-blue wizard's cloak, trimmed in gold, and several sizes too large for him. But then, modern-day Withering Wallop on the Wold is home to the annual Midsummer Madness Wizarding and Witchcraft Festival. So it's probably the only town in the world where, in the middle of summer, there are more people dressed as wizards and witches than there are, well, normal people.

He stared in awe at the colourful buildings lining both sides of the lane: the Enchanted Cave Cafe, the Charms and Enchantments Bazaar, Crystals and Cauldrons, Cat and Coven Clothes, the Market of Myths and Magic, Tricks and Trinkets Galore. Almost every merchant sold magikal goods.

Wilfred had heard many fabulous tales from travelling merchants, about strange and distant lands, and Wincewart often whiled away the cold, dark nights in the cave weaving magikal stories and conjuring mysterious pictures in the fire. Maybe that was why he felt strangely at home?

Wincewart would give his eye teeth to be here, he thought. But thinking of his master made him suddenly realise what he had done. He, Wilfred the Wise, had travelled to another place *by magik*! Even Wincewart had never done that.

'Frogs' warts!' he yelled happily, leaping up and down. 'Truly I must be a most powerful wizard!'

'I'm sure you are, dear, but could you move over so I can get by with my shopping trolley?' said an elderly woman trying to get into the Enchanted Cave Cafe.

Wilfred grabbed her arm. 'Thou do not understand! I have travelled *by scrying glass* from another land!'

'I don't care if you've come on the number sixteen bus from another planet,' she replied. 'I still can't get by. And let go of my arm!' she finished threateningly.

Hastily Wilfred moved out of her way and bowed apologetically.

The tormenting smell of hot food wafted up his nose as she opened the cafe door, and Wilfred's stomach rumbled louder than a snoring dragon. But he had no coins and nothing but the clothes he stood up in – oh, and a Bag of Bees magik charm. (To be fair, he hadn't exactly planned the trip. He'd only been hoping for a sneaky peek into the future.)

Wilfred pressed his face against the glass of the cafe window. 'Sheeps' sneezes and dragons' droppings! I shall starve to death!' he groaned.

Drooling hungrily at the food, Wilfred realised he didn't actually recognise much of it. But he wasn't going to let that worry him. He was starving. He felt like he hadn't eaten in a thousand years. (Well, technically, he *hadn't* eaten for a thousand years.)

So he let his grumbling belly follow his nose into the Enchanted Cave Cafe. A serving woman was dishing out food and drinks, and a kitchen girl about his age, with dark curly hair and a black hat, was helping her.

Wilfred was just about to pluck up the courage to ask if he could earn a hunk of bread when, to his astonishment, the girl casually put a drinking chalice under a metal box, pressed some magical symbols and conjured out a stream of hot liquid!

'Toads' earlobes!' gasped Wilfred. 'How did thou do that? Art thou a witch?'

'No! Why? Art thou a wizard?' joked the girl, eyeing Wilfred's (or rather Wincewart's) dark blue cloak with its magical symbols.

'I be merely an apprentice,' smiled Wilfred modestly, 'but did thou not enchant a drink into the chalice by magik?'

'Sure, watch!' laughed the girl, and did it again. 'Abracadabra!' Then, realising she now had a spare drink, she handed it to Wilfred. 'Try that. It's the best hot chocolate in town!'

'Hot-shock-lick'

Cautiously, Wilfred took the cup and sniffed it. Then he took a sip, and gasped. Compared to the food he usually ate (bitter rye bread, salty cheeses, nettle soup and soggy mangel-wurzels) the sweetness came as a surprise – well, more of a shock.

'What did thou call this?' he asked.

The girl shot him a funny look, then said: 'Er . . . hot chocolate?'

'I like this hot-shock-lick,' said Wilfred, adding, with great respect, 'Truly thou art mightily skilled.' Suddenly his eyes lit up and a lopsided cheerful grin broke out on his grubby face. 'Dost thou need a servant, my lady?'

The girl laughed out loud. 'One: I'm not "your lady", I'm Bel!' She grinned. 'But two: sure, I could do with a servant!'

'I thank thee, my lady Bel,' said Wilfred. Then, remembering his manners bowed politely and

added, 'That be a noble name. Mine be Wilfred. Wilfred the Wise,' he finished proudly.

'Cool name,' replied Bel. 'Goes with the outfit.'

Wilfred was baffled, but he smiled politely.

Bel assumed Wilfred was probably a young magician like her. *He certainly looks the part, and he acts it too,* she thought, impressed.

'So are you here for the festival?' she asked.

'Festival?' queried Wilfred.

'Yeah, the Midsummer Madness Wizarding and Witchcraft Festival.'

Wilfred's eyes lit up. 'Thou has a Midsummer Merrymaking of Magik and Mages here?'

'Isn't that why you're here, and all togged up like Gandalf?' laughed Bel. 'Or do you always dress like that?'

Wilfred didn't know how to answer, since he certainly didn't usually dress like a wizard – he wouldn't be allowed to. And he'd never heard of Gandalf.

'Have you come far?' she was asking.

Wilfred puffed up importantly, but tried to look modest at the same time. It wasn't easy. 'My lady, I have come a very great way from a distant land.'

Blimey, he's good, thought Bel, assuming Wilfred

was still pretending to be in character. *Maybe I ought to invent a stage persona as B-Dazzle? And a cool line in matching banter?* She'd work on it. But right now she decided it would be professional, and fun, to play along. 'Well, in that case, thou art very welcome, Wilfred the Wise!'

Wilfred's grubby face grinned.

The serving woman came over to dump a pile of dirty plates by the dishwasher.

'Mum, this is Wilfred,' said Bel.

'Wilfred *"the Wise"*,' he corrected, bowing respectfully to the serving woman.

'He's my servant!' grinned Bel.

'Your servant?' Gloria burst out laughing. (Which, as a matter of fact, is precisely what Wincewart would have done if he'd heard Wilfred's next sentence.)

'I can work hard!' claimed Wilfred eagerly, pushing his grimy mop of hair off his face and managing to look at least keen, if not clean. 'And I do not want coins, only food,' he added.

Gloria ran her eye over Wilfred. He was a bit mucky, but then so were lots of the kids at the festival. She was used to the annual rag-tag mob of witches and wizards, and their assorted offspring.

He seemed a nice enough lad and was obviously into magic, which would, she thought, be good for Bel, who was missing her mates. She wondered if Bel was regretting turning down the invitation to go camping with them. *Probably not,* she guessed, since wild horses wouldn't keep Bel away from the festival, or anything remotely magical.

'Well in that case, wash your hands – *thoroughly* – help Bel load the dishwasher, and I'll give you a bacon butty. Fair?'

Wilfred hesitated. He knew what bacon was, but he didn't like the sound of a 'butty'. He wondered if it might hurt, and if so, exactly where and how much. But, judging by the way Bel was smiling at him, she obviously thought it was a good idea.

So, bowing humbly, he said, 'I thank thee, my lady.'

'Er . . . you can call me Gloria,' smiled Bel's mum, going off to collect another tray of dirty dishes.

'Come on then, servant!' ordered Bel at the dishwasher. 'Scrub up. Then you can pass me the plates and I'll stack.'

Chapter Six

It does not go well at the castle

Meanwhile, a thousand years ago (or a millennium, if you prefer) Wincewart arrived at the magnificent castle that stood on the hill above the small medieval village of Wallop in the Wold. Bertram perched precariously on his hat.

The castle had only recently been finished. It had taken teams of stonemasons and carpenters a good many years to build, but now Lord Wallop's flags fluttered on the lofty towers and battlements. A series of extraordinarily menacing gargoyles, with wonky noses and outsized ears, glared down from the walls. (Rumour had it they were based on Lord Wallop's mother-in-law.) An enormous and downright ostentatious shield bearing the crest of the Wallop dynasty (crossed long swords and a flying wild boar, complete with tusks) hung over the stone gateway.

The mighty mage strode into the gatehouse, raised his staff, and pounded dramatically on the huge iron-studded oak doors. 'Open, I say, in the name of Wincewart the Withering, Castle Mage, Soothsaying Sage and the greatest wizard in all Wallop in the Wold!' he bellowed commandingly.

To his enormous embarrassment, the mighty doors, which, had he been wearing his dragon's claw talisman, would have majestically swung wide, lurched open a couple of feet and then stopped.

'Hags' henbane!' swore Wincewart, giving the doors a mighty kick and pushing through them, hoping no one had noticed. But Bertram the Beady had. He cocked his head to one side, thoughtfully.

Inside the castle courtyard it was utter chaos. A hundred or so people were getting ready for the Midsummer Merrymaking of Magik and Mages. Well, that was what they were supposed to be doing.

Most of them were running around like headless chickens. The butcher and the cook were arguing hotly about where to put the hog roast. The ale keeper was setting up his tented beer table right in the middle of the courtyard and getting in everyone's way. Half a dozen barrels had tumbled off the back of a horse-drawn cart and demolished a handful of stalls. The rest of the traders were yelling threats and abuse at the carter, at each other and even at the horse. (The horse being the only one who didn't yell back.)

'It does not go well, methinks,' commented Bertram wryly.

'It does not,' agreed Wincewart.

Lord Wallop

Wincewart winced as the cook threw a punch at the butcher. Fortunately he didn't get to see what happened next, because just at that moment Lord Wallop, the owner of the castle, appeared.

'Wincewart! Thank goodness thou art here,' he bellowed.

'Oh, so *he* can call thee Wincewart, but not I?' hissed Bertram jealously in Wincewart's ear.

'Yes, and shut thy beak!' hissed the wizard back.

'My Lord,' cried Wincewart, bowing deeply. 'Thou summoned me.'

Lord Wallop was a gurt great bear of a man. He was almost as tall as he was wide. And that says a lot. He had a huge red beard and a head full of shaggy red hair. (He also had a head full of fleas, but then everybody did in those days, so don't judge.)

'I need thou to sort out this rabble!' bellowed Lord Wallop, waving at the surrounding pandemonium. Then turning back to Wincewart, he suddenly exclaimed, 'Whatever have thou done to thy beard?'

'A small enchantment did not go to plan,' replied the wizard, waving his hand dismissively.

'Oh, right. Well, there are but two days until the merrymaking is upon us and I have invited many lords and ladies, and I wish to impress them mightily.'

Bertram squawked and fluttered off in alarm as Lord Wallop flung a huge arm around Wincewart's shoulders and bawled in his ear.

'I told them I have the greatest wizard in all the land.'

'Thou art too kind, my lord,' replied Wincewart.

'What?' snapped Lord Wallop. 'Art thou *not* the greatest?' He shot Wincewart a dangerous look. In all honesty, he would have replaced Wincewart in a candle's snuff if he could find a better wizard – and Wincewart knew that only too well.

'Oh, verily I be,' spluttered Wincewart hurriedly.

'So, tell me, what wondrous magical spectacle has thou planned?'

'My noble lord, I will conjure a marvel no magician has ever done before.'

'I would expect no less. But what, exactly, will that marvel be?' persisted Lord Wallop.

The wizard paused theatrically then said, 'I shall make myself . . . disappear into thin air!'

He was rewarded with a gasp of astonishment. 'Can thou do that?'

Wincewart bowed his head modestly.

Most wizards worth their salt could make objects and animals disappear. But for a wizard to make *himself* vanish was much harder. Because once the wizard had disappeared, then he wasn't where he started from to bring himself back – if you see what I mean. (Which you might not, since my explanation might be a little confusing, but it's the best I can do. Sorry.)

Anyhow, Lord Wallop was hugely impressed and rubbed his hands together greedily. 'I look forward to it, and so will mine guests, and mine dear lady wife!' he finished pointedly. 'Well, I leave all this in thine hands,' he bellowed, waving vaguely at the chaos in the courtyard. Then he thumped Wincewart heartily on the back again, and strode off.

Bertram fluttered back to perch on the wizened wizard's shoulder, and eyed him sceptically. '*Can* thou actually make thyself disappear without thy talisman?'

'I will not have to. Wilfred will find it.'

'But what if he does not?'

'It will be in the cave somewhere,' said Wincewart casually.

'But what if it be not in the cave?' persisted Bertram.

'The boy has not the skill to conjure the talisman out of the cave. He has not the skill to conjure anything anywhere!' retorted Wincewart.

Which just goes to show how wrong even the most powerful wizard in all of eleventh century Wallop in the Wold can be.

Chapter Seven

Withering Wallop in the Wold

Right at that moment, Wilfred was greedily scoffing a bacon butty, slurping another 'hot-shock-lick' and following Bel down the main street. He was blissfully unaware that he had an improbably large hot-chocolatey moustache, which Bel was too polite to mention as she led him on a grand tour of the town. (But I'm not, so I have.)

There wasn't a great deal to see, but she figured showing Wilfred around would be more fun than clearing tables at the Enchanted Cave Cafe. A lot more fun. With his weird sense of humour, he was turning out to be hilarious.

'Behind us,' she waved vaguely over her shoulder, 'is the swimming pool – not quite Olympic size, of course. And then there's the supermarket . . . the tourist office . . . and the chemist.'

Wilfred traipsed enthusiastically after her, utterly baffled but smiling and nodding in a way he hoped looked wise. Strange words flew from Bel's lips like bees from a hive.

'This is the post office,' she announced. Then, walking up to the doors, she cried, 'Shazam!' To Wilfred's astonishment, the doors opened *all by themselves*. He was speechless, but Bel had already moved on, so he hurried after her.

By the time he caught up she was waiting to cross the road. She pressed a button on the colour changing lamp nearby and, to his amazement, the lights promptly turned red and the lantern let out several high-pitched squeaks, as if it were alive. Almost immediately, everyone obediently stopped their strange metal carts to let Bel cross.

'My lady! Did thou command everyone to stop for thee?'

'I did indeed, Wilfred the Wise,' she joked.

Turning back to face the crossing she added, 'Watch and learn!' and she clicked her fingers, pointed at the lights and cried, 'Hocus pocus!'

Wilfred was awestruck. The lamps not only turned from red to orange, but started flashing!

'I be dazzled by thy skills,' he said.

'Of course you are! I'm B-Dazzle – and you've been B-Dazzled!' grinned Bel.

She carried on, stopping outside an ancient stone building. 'This is the library. It's dead old.' She pushed open the huge oak door for Wilfred to look inside.

'Dung beetles' droppings!' He'd only ever seen one book in his whole life (Wincewart's grimoire). He gazed at the endless rows of bookshelves. 'Verily, thou must have all the books in the world in there! Have thou read them all?'

'Oh verily! Every one, and many times,' joked Bel, not thinking for one minute that Wilfred would take her seriously. But, looking at him, he seemed to be doing just that, and with a perfectly straight face. *He's a brilliant actor*, she thought.

'How long have you been doing the "Wilfred the Wise" routine?' she asked. 'It's very good.'

Wilfred looked at her blankly, not understanding

her at all. But he didn't want to seem stupid so he answered vaguely, 'Oh . . . for a goodly while.'

Bel seemed satisfied with that, and walked along and turned the corner. Wilfred followed eagerly.

'And now we come to the high point of the tour!' she announced with mock pride. 'The most famous part of the entire town.' She made a grand gesture towards a building at the top of the hill that stood before them. 'The castle!'

Wallop Castle

'Be that it?' laughed Wilfred tactlessly.

'Oh, charming!' retorted Bel.

To be fair to Wilfred, it didn't look like any castle he'd ever seen. It looked more like a pile of rubble, although there were a few bits that might have been sections of a battlement, walls and a gateway.

Methinks they are still building it, he thought, and realising he had offended Bel he replied with what was for him, unusual tact. 'It will be magnificent when they have finished it.'

To his astonishment, Bel burst out laughing.

Confused, Wilfred turned to look at the castle again. Was it some sort of jest? It seemed strangely familiar to him, but then most castles were built out of great lumps of stone on the tops of hills. He looked more closely and made out a couple of extraordinarily menacing gargoyles with wonky noses and outsized ears. On the gatehouse was a shabby shield faintly depicting a pair of crossed swords and a flying wild boar, complete with tusks.

He'd seen them before somewhere, he was sure. It took a few seconds while he remembered where . . . then he reeled in shock.

'What be this castle called?' he gasped.

'Wallop Castle.'

'And what be this village called?'

'It's not a village, it's a town, and it's Withering Wallop in the Wold,' grinned Bel. To be honest, she wondered if he wasn't taking his act just a bit far.

'Bats' buttocks!' cried Wilfred and his hands flew to his mouth as he sank to his knees on the pavement.

'What has become of my lord's castle?' he wailed.

Bel shot him a look. *Seriously?* she thought. *He really is going over the top a bit now.*

But poor Wilfred was genuinely horrified.

The magnificent castle that had once stood so

60

imposingly at the top of the hill, now lay in ruins. Its mighty towers had tumbled to the ground. Stones from the broken battlements lay strewn across the hillside. Much of the great wall had crumbled to rubble and it was overgrown with grass and weeds.

A dreadful, terrible thought struck him. Was this, like so many other catastrophes, all *his* fault? Had he somehow, by using Ye Olde Yet Effective Runic Foretelling Spell, destroyed the castle? And worse, was his master, Wincewart the Withering, in it at the time?

'Wild boars' belches! What have I done?' he wailed, and was staggered when Bel hooted with laughter.

When be it?

Appalled, Wilfred gawped at the remains of Lord Wallop's castle and ran his hand despairingly through his scruffy hair. 'How did this happen? Did thou see it fall?' he asked Bel.

'Wilf – it fell down hundreds of years ago, of course I didn't see it fall!'

Wilfred frowned, struggling to understand what Bel had just said.

Despite being a hopeless apprentice, Wilfred was actually quite smart. It was just that the enormity of what Bel had said was taking time to sink in. Slowly the confusion clouding his face cleared. And eventually he asked Bel a simple but important question.

'When be it?'

Bel looked at her watch. 'Quarter to three.'

Wilfred stared at the strange little sundial on her wrist.

Seeing him look so puzzled, Bel joked: 'You know, as in the big hand is on the nine and the little hand is nearly at three o'clock!'

'No, not the hour, I know that by the sun! What year be it?'

She laughed. 'It's 2016! Has been since January!'

'2016? Art thou sure?'

'Duh . . . yes.'

'Not 1016?'

'Ha! Hilarious,' cried Bel but then yelped as Wilfred grabbed her arm in a painfully crushing grip.

'My lady, thou do not understand. I have travelled, *by scrying glass, one thousand years into the future*! Not even my master himself could do that!'

'No, I don't suppose he could. But let go of my arm, before it falls off.'

Wilfred did so.

The Legend of Wincewart the Withering

'My master will be so proud of me!' he exclaimed. 'Have thou heard of Wincewart the Withering?' he added casually.

'Are you joking?' retorted Bel. 'If it wasn't for Wincewart the Withering, the town wouldn't be called Withering Wallop in the Wold!

'*Withering* Wallop in the Wold?' gasped Wilfred, astounded to learn that his master was so important they had actually re-named the village after him.

But Bel was still talking. 'And there wouldn't be a Midsummer Madness Wizarding and Witchcraft Festival every year!' She waved at the mass of tents and people sprawled all over the hillside by the remains of the castle.

'And the streets wouldn't be full wizards and witches and barking mad tourists . . . and my mum wouldn't run a teashop called the Enchanted Cave Cafe . . . and my dad wouldn't have a shop selling more magical charms and trinkets than you can shake a broomstick at! Everyone knows the Legend of Wincewart.'

'The '*Legend* of Wincewart'?' repeated Wilfred, humbled to hear his master had also become the subject of folklore. 'I do not.'

So Bel told him the ancient story, handed down through the centuries. It was about a long-lost cave the wizard had lived in but had enchanted, so that no one would be able to find it. Some said it was full of treasure, others said it housed a sleeping dragon, whilst others claimed Wincewart himself was buried there. In all honesty, most people in Withering Wallop in the Wold didn't believe in the legend for one second, never mind a thousand years. But it was *very* good for business.

'Hang on, if you don't know about Wincewart, then how come you're here at the festival?'

Wilfred visibly puffed up with pride. 'My lady, I did not know the *legend*, but I do know Wincewart *himself!*' He paused for effect. 'I be his apprentice.'

'Wilf, you're brilliant!' laughed Bel.

'I be,' insisted Wilfred indignantly. 'I do not jest!'

But that just set Bel off again. 'You're very funny, and it's a really smart idea for an act. And I love the way you keep it up.'

Wilfred shot her a very confused look.

'Come on, fancy an ice cream?' said Bel, heading off.

Wilfred gave up trying to convince her, hitched up Wincewart's cloak and followed her.

Chapter Eight

The Frozen Goblet

The Frozen Goblet ice-cream parlour in the High Street sold about twenty different flavours, six types of cornets and dozens of fancy toppings. Wilfred, never having encountered ice cream, was completely overwhelmed. So Bel bought him a double cornet with a scoop of mint choc chip and a scoop of cookie dough, topped with candy sprinkles.

'Alas, I have no coins,' he mumbled in embarrassment as she paid.

'Don't worry about it,' shrugged Bel, handing him

the cornet. 'You can buy me one another time.'

'Another time?' breathed Wilfred in awe. 'My lady, can thou travel through time?'

'Not right now, my TARDIS has broken down!' grinned Bel.

Wilfred was just about to ask what a 'tardis' was, but the strange thing that Bel had given him was melting, like a candle. Only cold. He watched, fascinated. 'What did thou call this?'

'Ice cream,' replied Bel with a perfectly straight face.

Eye scream? wondered Wilfred. He took an enormous bite and three seconds later a massive bout of brain-freeze kicked him in the forehead. Wilfred thought his skull and eye sockets were going to explode.

'Maggots' mumps!' he cried, 'I see why thou call it "eye scream"! Mine eyes, they scream in pain!'

'Serves you right for taking such a huge bite!' snorted Bel.

Ye Basic Colour-Changing Enchantment

They sat on a bench overlooking the castle grounds, slurping their ice creams. Preparations for the festival were in full flow. Half a dozen enormous marquees were in various stages of construction, and the grass was littered with scaffolding and plastic chairs for building banks of seats.

Men in yellow hi-vis jackets were rigging a stage, while others wheeled mobile light units off a lorry or reeled out miles of electric cable. Half the hillside was covered with people picnicking and putting up tents.

Wilfred had gone very quiet. 'My lady, I have no coins and no way of getting any. So I will never be able to pay thou back,' he said, embarrassed.

Bel glanced at him and he looked so apologetic she felt sorry for him. Although her parents weren't exactly rolling in money, they did give her an allowance. She had to work for it, of course, but she supposed that was fair enough since her parents had to work to get the money in the first place.

So she said, 'No worries, I can always find money when I need it,' and, secretly slipping a pound coin up her sleeve, she pretended to 'find' it behind Wilfred's ear. She opened her palm to show him the coin. 'See?'

Wilfred was delighted, and immensely relieved. 'May I have it?' he asked, taking the coin.

'Sure,' shrugged Bel.

'I thank thee most humbly. Truly thou art a skilled enchantress.'

'Nah, lots of magicians can do that.'

'Well, I cannot. *And* thou can conjure up hot-shock-licks, and enchant dishes clean!'

'That's not magic! That's technology!'

'Thou art being modest!' insisted Wilfred. 'I know I be only a humble apprentice but I do have some skills,' and he looked around eagerly to see what he could do to impress her. (You would think that since Wilfred's attempt to impress Wincewart had had *such* disastrous consequences he might be a bit less keen to try showing off again. I mean, I know it was a thousand years ago, but even so.)

His eyes settled on the coloured lanterns at the sides of the lane behind them. Clutching his Bag of Bees in one hand and pointing confidently at the lights with the other, he uttered the words of Ye Basic Colour-Changing Enchantment.

It was a very, very bad idea.

There was a flash of light, a shower of colourful sparks and a noise like thunder crackling right next to them.

SKEREEEECH . . . BEEEEEEP, BLAAAARE!

Bel dropped her ice cream and stared in disbelief. All the traffic lights had gone green *at the same time* . . .

Three cars, a parcel delivery truck and a double decker bus collided in the middle of the road with an almighty

KERRAAAAASHHHHH!

'Adders' bladders!' gulped Wilfred. 'Did I do that?'

By scrying glass!

Wilfred and Bel watched as the drivers clambered out of their vehicles, yelling and swearing at each other and waving their arms about furiously. (It's amazing the scale and quantity of spectacular drama the average traffic crash can produce – without causing any major damage to the vehicles, or any minor injuries to the passengers at all.)

Bel wasn't at all sure what she had seen. The traffic lights had *all* turned green – and stayed green

– that was obvious, but had Wilfred actually made that happen? *No,* she thought, *that would be impossible.* In the distance she could hear sirens, so pulling Wilfred by the sleeve of his cloak she said, 'I think we should disappear.'

'Can thou make things disappear?' he cried, astounded. If Bel could do that, she must be as powerful as Wincewart the Withering himself!

'Yes. I can, kind of,' replied Bel, thinking about how she could hide her phone up her sleeve.

'But, my lady, I do not want to vanish!' Wilfred wailed. But he realised Bel just seemed to mean they should move away. So he did as she bade him, *but with great respect.*

'Where are you from?' Bel asked as they cut down a side alley.

'I be from here. From Wallop in the Wold.'

'Then how come I haven't met you before?'

Withering Wallop in the Wold is a small town and there's only one school, so it's almost impossible not to meet everyone who's about your age – possibly several times a day.

'Because I be from the past.' said Wilfred simply. 'I told thee.'

'Be serious!'

'But I do be serious. I came from one thousand years ago,' he insisted.

Bel laughed. 'Okay . . .' she said. 'In that case, how did you get here?'

Wilfred took a deep breath, paused for effect and said: 'By scrying glass.'

'What, like a crystal ball?'

'Verily so,' replied Wilfred.

'Ha! Awesome!' laughed Bel. 'And I love the way you say "scrying glass" instead of "crystal ball". You must have done a lot research. Most people haven't even heard of a scrying glass.'

'But then most people be not wizards!' he grinned.

'True!'

'Does thou have a scrying glass?' he asked casually.

'No, but I know a man who does!' laughed Bel.

Chapter Nine

Lady Wallop's Requests

Meanwhile (or possibly a very long time ago – whichever way you want to look at it) up at Lord Wallop's castle in the Middle Ages, Wincewart was beginning to regret making Wilfred stay behind in the hermit cave.

There was an enormous amount to do for the merrymaking and without Wilfred to run errands, fend off endless queries from stallholders, and generally fetch and carry, it was all falling to

Wincewart. Bertram was with him of course, but a raven can only do so much.

All in all, Wincewart was having a very trying morning, which was made worse – *much worse* – when a strident voice pierced the warm summer air, shrieking his name and stopping him in his tracks.

'Wince-WART!' screeched the voice. It belonged to the Lady Wallop. She was an improbably tiny but impressively forceful woman, who ran the castle with a rod of iron. Quite literally, some said, swearing they had the bruises to prove it.

Wincewart flinched. Bertram fluttered off in alarm. The gaggle of stallholders, who had been clustering around badgering the wizard, nipped off sharpish.

Lady Wallop scampered across the castle yard towards Wincewart, hitching up the hem of her expensive silk gown to enable her tiny feet to scurry her along.

'I have a small number of simple magikal tasks I need thee to do,' she squeaked. Then, as she noticed the state of Wincewart, she suddenly exclaimed, 'Whatever has thou done to thy beard?'

'A small enchantment did not go to plan,' replied the wizard, waving his hand dismissively.

'Oh, right. Well, I have brought thou a quill pen and parchment to make a list,' she added, pointedly handing them to Wincewart, together with a worryingly large flask of ink.

Wincewart's heart sank. Gloomily he sat on the edge of a cart to write. Bertram settled on a nearby stall and watched with one beady eye.

'I be a wizard, not a scribe!'

The Lady Wallop, it turned out, had a very long list, and some of the enchantments were far from simple.

Could she have a pair of silver slippers that could dance on their own? And would he just turn her dress bright blue, to match the sky? And could he enchant the gargoyles above the castle gate to speak so that they could welcome the guests as they arrived? And could he also . . .

Frantically scribbling away, Wincewart suddenly raised his hand, begging her to pause. 'My lady, these art not simple enchantments,' he protested, 'And there art so many . . .'

A dangerous look darkened Lady Wallop's eyes. 'My sister's mage Ignatius the Ingenious can do all of these and more besides,' she said. 'Art thou telling me he be better than thee? Methinks Lord Wallop would want to know if that be true!'

'No, no no,' replied Wincewart hastily, and he beckoned to his familiar. 'Bertram, thou must go back to the cave and fetch Wilfred. I be a wizard, not a scribe!' he blustered, shooting a pained look from under his bushy eyebrows at Lady Wallop. Then, muttering softly behind his hand, he added to Bertram, 'And tell him to bring my dragon's claw talisman with him!'

'But what if he hath not found it, Wincewart?' cawed the raven quietly.

'Just tell him to come!' snapped Wincewart irritably, 'AND DO NOT CALL ME WINCEWART!' Bertram opened his jet-black wings and launched himself up gratefully into the clear blue summer sky, glad to escape the demanding Lady Wallop.

Wincewart the Weary

The Lady Wallop asks a lot, wants and lot, and worst of all, she talks a lot, thought Bertram, soaring over the castle walls and back to the cave to fetch Wilfred.

Landing in the entrance of the cave it was immediately obvious to the bird that Wilfred wasn't there. An eleventh century hermit cave is usually just the one room, and not a very large one at that.

The raven cawed Wilfred's name a couple of times – but there was no reply.

This be odd, he thought. Wilfred might be a bit of a clot-head, not to mention a complete liability as an apprentice, but Bertram doubted he would actually disobey Wincewart. The raven guessed Wilfred had just popped outside – perhaps to fetch firewood, or water.

So, spreading his wings he took off and scanned the surrounding countryside, coasting on the warm wind high above the cave. But he soon saw Wilfred was nowhere near-abouts. Somewhat surprised, he headed back to tell his master.

When Bertram got back to the castle, the small but forceful Lady Wallop was still dictating her demands. So he wisely decided to perch on the battlements well out of her way until after she'd finished – a fact that did not escape Wincewart's notice.

The wizard had resorted to bewitching the quill pen to write on its own. He'd had to enchant the parchment as well, to make it longer. Quite a bit longer, and now some of it lay rolled on the ground.

The Lady Wallop wanted a pie filled with twenty-four blackbirds that would fly out when it was cut open, a magical lute that could play by itself, and enchanted chalices that would instantly re-fill themselves with wine as the guests drank from them, and . . . on and on she went.

But her list finally ended, and the quill pen dropped exhausted onto the parchment with a pathetic little flutter.

'Well, I leave thee to it,' she exclaimed, whirling away. Wincewart could only nod weakly as she scuttled off, screaming for her husband. 'Wallop! WALLOP!' she shrieked.

As soon as she was safely gone, Bertram swooped down and landed on his master's shoulder.

'Coward!' sniffed Wincewart witheringly.

Bertram did not deny it. 'Master, I know not how to tell thee this, but the boy be not in the cave.'

Furiously snatching up the quill and parchment, Wincewart stormed out of the castle and down the hillside, cursing Wilfred to high heaven as he went.

'Did I not tell thee he was as much use as a hairy

wart on a wild boar's rump?' said Bertram, wobbling on his shoulder.

He was rewarded with an angry *harrumph!* in reply.

Wincewart the Furious

Striding into the cave, Wincewart made an impressively terrifying entrance, with his wizard cloak swirling dramatically around him – even though it was only his second best one. (What a shame his performance was wasted on an empty cave.)

'Wilfred!' he bellowed, loudly enough to make the dust swirl about the floor. There was, of course, no reply. 'WILFRED!' Under their grizzled brows, Wincewart's eyes scanned the cave.

He saw his red leather-bound grimoire lying open on the oak table, next to a purple spell candle, a dragon's scale. And – worst of all! – his favourite scrying glass on the floor *and inside a magik pentacle.*

'Clumsy oaf! How many times have I told him not to fool with mine things?' Sweeping the scrying glass up off the ground, Wincewart set it on the table before him. 'Crones' curses! When I get my hands on him I shall give him the horns of a goat, the ears of a march hare and the . . . the . . .' he tailed off, beside himself with fury and lost for words.

'The eyes of a slug? The teeth of a mule? The spines of a hedgehog?' offered Bertram helpfully.

'Verily! And much more besides. And then I will rip off his cloddish head altogether and pickle it in pig's pee and chicken poo!'

'Thou will have to find him first,' observed Bertram dryly.

'That will not be hard to do,' harrumphed Wincewart. Gathering a few ingredients together, he picked up the purple spell candle, lit and stood it on the table, and then reached for his scrying glass.

He sat down heavily in his chair and, clasping his scrying glass in both hands, looked into its depths and muttered the enchantment of Ye Very Ancient Seeing Spell:

'*Oh, crystal ball*
Thou can see all.
I command thee,

Reveal to me . . .

Where my good-for-nothing-disobedient-useless-lumpen-dolt-of-an-apprentice, do be.'

Slowly the glass flooded with inky swirls of deep-blue smoke. Wincewart watched intently, waiting for it to clear, and to show him where to find Wilfred.

Chapter Ten

Crystals and Cauldrons

CHIME, TINKLE, CHIME.

A set of small hanging bells jangled together as Bel opened the door to Crystals and Cauldrons. Wilfred followed her inside. Bel's dad had owned the shop since before she was born, and after so many years it was crammed to the ceiling with all kinds of weird and wonderful stuff, all with a magical theme.

'Hey, dudette!' called Jon from the till, where he was sorting out a tray of glass trinket bottles full of coloured bewitching dust.

'Dad, this is Wilfred,' said Bel, going over.

'Wilfred *the Wise*,' Wilfred reminded her sheepishly.

'Wilfred, huh? Cool name, dude,' smiled Jon.

'It be a joy to meet thee, my noble lord Dad. Be thou well?' asked Wilfred politely and with a small bow.

Without batting an eyelid, Jon bowed in return and replied, 'I am indeed well, kind sir, and I thank thee for asking.' After all, you can't run a magical goods shop in a town teaming with modern day witches and wizards without meeting some pretty eccentric customers. (Well, barking mad ones really. Especially those who are genuinely convinced they *are* witches and wizards, complete with pointed hats and hooded cloaks, staffs and broomsticks and magic powers!)

Bel grinned at her dad. She'd have bet a tenner that he and her new mate would get on. 'Wilf's interested in scrying glasses,' she told him.

'Awesome! They're over there – but hey, take your time, look around . . . !' he finished, waving his arms around expansively.

So much magik!

Wilfred wandered around the shop in wide-eyed amazement. 'Piglets' pimples!' he exclaimed, drifting from one colourful display to another, gingerly picking up objects and carefully putting them back. *Wincewart would give his eye teeth to be here*, he thought. (Actually, given how furious the wizard was right now, it might be more accurate to say Wincewart would have given *Wilfred's* eye teeth – or indeed, many other parts of his apprentice's body.)

Humbly Wilfred eyed the brightly polished crystals and gemstones, the coloured spell candles, wooden pentacles and charm scrolls. He marvelled at a display of potion bottles of all shapes, sizes and colours. There was a rack of 'Bees in a Bag' magic charms strung on leather cords (very similar to his own), and countless amulets and necklaces. The sheer quantity overawed him. He was, unusually for him, speechless.

Drawn to a display of decorated chalices with straight sides and curved handles, he picked one up carefully. It had a witch on a broomstick painted on one side.

'What be this strange object?' he asked.

'It's a mug!' said Bel, rolling her eyes at Jon, who grinned back.

'A mug,' repeated Wilfred, nodding in what he hoped was a wise manner, and putting it back.

'That's one cool dude,' remarked Jon approvingly to Bel.

'Yeah, he's hilarious. And he's really into his magic act. He stays in character the *whole* time. It's really impressive, and he must have done loads of research.'

'I'm guessing he's here for the festival,' said Jon.

'I think so,' said Bel, but actually wishing Wilfred would be around for the whole summer, if not longer. It'd be great to have someone to practise magic with. Someone who'd really get what she was trying to do, and criticise the flaws in her tricks honestly.

Wilfred had found the scrying glasses. One in particular caught his eye. Larger than the others, it came in its own wooden box. It reminded him of Wincewart's. He picked it up. Suddenly, to his astonishment (actually, make that utter terror), it filled with inky swirls of deep-blue smoke. He nearly dropped it. Spellbound, he watched the smoke clear to reveal the hugely magnified image of a single eye. In fact, every single crystal ball on the shelf was filled with the same outsized, piercing eyeball. He froze, trapped in their all-seeing gaze.

Ye Very Ancient Seeing Spell

A thousand years away, in his dim and modest hermit cave, Wincewart sat with hunched shoulders and furrowed brow, holding his precious scrying glass in his cupped hands.

His grizzled eye peered into the glass orb, and (out of a dozen or more crystal balls) straight into the inside of Crystals and Cauldrons, in what was (unbeknownst to him) another millennium.

The wizard's eye blinked and swept around the interior of the shop. It could not believe what it saw – an entire room, stacked floor-to-ceiling with priceless magikal goods.

'By the nose hairs of Hildebrand the Hideous!' gasped Wincewart.

'What?' cawed Bertram. 'What can thou see?'

'Thou will not believe me! There be a bright cavern full of more magikal objects and charms than thou can imagine! There cannot be such wealth! And yet I see it with mine own eyes!'

'But can thou see Wilfred?' squawked his familiar impatiently, and more to the point.

Wincewart peered back into the glass again . . . and saw Wilfred peering back! Not only could he see his apprentice clearly, but he could see that he was wearing a long midnight-blue cloak with gold trimming, which was several sizes too large for him. It was Wincewart's best wizarding cloak!

'Wilfred!' bellowed Wincewart angrily. 'WILFRED!'

Eyeballs

Ganders' gizzards! Wilfred jumped guiltily.

'WILFRED!' rapped the voice again. It sounded strangely thin and weedy.

Gobbling gooses! He'd know that voice anywhere. He gulped, and eyed the eyeballs in the scrying glasses fearfully.

'I see thee! Thou cannot hide!' squeaked Wincewart. 'Thou art staring at me like a frightened rabbit and opening and shutting thy mouth like a haddock!' (Which was an extremely accurate description of his apprentice.)

'Master!' cried Wilfred.

'Where art thou?' demanded the wizard's voice.

'Thou will not believe me!' exclaimed Wilfred excitedly. 'I have travelled *to the future*! And by scrying glass, all on mine own!' he finished proudly.

Wilfred was right. Wincewart didn't believe him, not for a second. In fact not in a thousand years would the wizard believe his dunderhead of an apprentice could achieve anything as remarkable as that. 'Do not lie to me!' he snapped.

'But, master –'

Wincewart interrupted him furiously. 'Do thou take me for a fool? Thou could not possibly do as thou claim. And why art thou wearing mine best cloak?' he barked angrily.

'Um . . .' stammered Wilfred hopelessly, pushing his hand through his hair.

'And, more to the point, have thou found mine talisman?'

'Er . . .' stalled Wilfred, looking wildly around him.

'I take it thou has not!' raged Wincewart. 'Yet I

forbade thee to leave the cave until thou had found it! When I get my hands on thee I shall turn thee into . . .'

But Wilfred didn't wait to hear what dire and dreadful fate his furious master had in store for him. Panic-stricken, he thrust the scrying glass back onto the shelf and legged it to join Bel and Jon at the till.

'Wilfred. WILFRED!' screeched Wincewart's tinny little voice, but Wilfred had disappeared.

How dare he!

Back in ye olden times, Wincewart stormed furiously up and down the cave, his cloak billowing theatrically around him like dark clouds around a lightning bolt.

'How dare he disobey me!' roared the wizard. 'HOW DARE HE!'

Bertram fluttered onto the table in front of him, and put his head to one side, giving the wizard a sharp look with his beady eye. 'And did he not lie to thee too?'

'He did!' agreed Wincewart, nodding readily. 'He told me he had travelled to the future. By scrying glass!'

'Can *thou* travel to the future?' asked Bertram.

'Nay! I cannot!' retorted Wincewart.

The raven strutted back and forth across the table in front of Wincewart. 'But if a mighty wizard and skilled sorcerer like thou can not do it, why wouldst a lumpen, doltish, clumsy, clot-headed apprentice like Wilfred the Unwise think that thou wouldst believe he can?' he cawed.

'Because he is a lumpen, doltish, clumsy, clot-headed . . . idiot!' snapped Wincewart. 'Methinks he is hiding somewhere, too scared to face me.'

'Methinks he has run away,' squawked his familiar.

By the oaths of Oswald the Outrageous

Wincewart shot the bird a scandalised look. That idea would never have occurred to him in a thousand years. An eleventh century apprentice was pretty much dependent on his master for everything.

To the wizard's certain knowledge, Wilfred had nothing but the clothes he stood up in – oh, and his Bag of Bees magik charm, of course.

'But he be penniless!' he cried.

'He be also witless,' scoffed Bertram. 'He certainly

be not worth the leather in his boots, or the tunic on his back. And he *definitely* be not worth the splendid blue-and-gold wizarding cloak that he hath taken with him.'

Wincewart slammed both his fists onto the table in fury, sucked in his breath and turned such an impressively deep purple that Bertram feared he would explode. He swore by the oaths of Oswald the Outrageous to tan Wilfred's hide, roast his rump and batter his buttocks. He threatened to turn him into a stone gargoyle with a monstrous face and a waterspout mouth. He declared that plague, pestilence and pox would be visited upon him in equal and agonising quantities.

'Thou will not be able to do that if he be not here!' cackled Bertram wisely.

Wincewart harrumphed loudly. 'Ha! Thou will see. He will be home before supper, with his tail between his legs like a scolded pup!'

Chapter Eleven

The Remarkable Disappearing Coin Trick

Thoroughly rattled from his run-in with Wincewart, Wilfred rushed over to Bel so quickly that he knocked over a stack of coloured spell candles.

'Hey, careful, dude!' said Jon mildly.

'I do be sorry. I be a clumsy dolt, and a lumpen oaf!' said Wilfred and, giving Jon a lopsided sheepish grin, he scrabbled on the floor on his hands and knees to pick them up. 'Thou must be a mighty wizard, Lord Dad,' he added, carefully putting the candles back on the stand.

'Alas no,' replied Jon, 'I'm only a humble merchant. But Bel's an awesome magician. I reckon she should try out her magic at the festival.'

'Thou should, my lady!' nodded Wilfred enthusiastically.

'Don't you start!' exclaimed Bel.

'Chillax! It's a cool idea!' said Jon.

'No! It's not! You don't "try out your magic" on your public. You wait till you're ready to . . . to . . .'

'Knock 'em dead . . . rock their socks off . . . astound, astonish and amaze them?' grinned Jon.

'"B-Dazzle" them,' said Bel.

'But you will bedazzle them!' protested her dad.

'Verily, thou will!' exclaimed Wilfred.

'How do you know? You've no idea what I can do,' said Bel to Wilfred.

'So show him!' cried Jon. 'He's not "the public". He's just Wilfred.'

'Wilfred "*the Wise*",' corrected Wilfred, yet again.

'What does it matter if you make a mistake?' said Jon.

'Indeed, my lady. I make them all the time,' nodded Wilfred earnestly (and honestly).

'So do I,' confessed Bel, 'But that doesn't mean I want other people to see!'

'My lady, I beg thee,' pleaded Wilfred. And his grubby face looked at her so imploringly she gave in.

'Oh, all right,' she groaned and, turning to Jon she held out her hand. 'Can you lend me a pound from the till?'

'No chance! I'm not falling for that one again,' grinned Jon, then added jokingly to Wilfred, 'Don't ever lend her any money. She'll make it disappear and you'll never see it again!'

Wilfred slid his hand into his pocket and clasped the coin Bel had given him. He was torn. It was the only coin he'd got, and probably the only one he'd ever be likely to get for a long time, but he desperately wanted to see Bel's magik.

'Oh, come on, Dad,' Bel grinned. 'Do you want me to show Wilf or not?'

Sighing theatrically, Jon opened the till and handed her a pound coin.

Bel held the coin in her right hand, showing it to Wilfred. 'Watch closely, and I will make this coin disappear into thin air,' she said.

Placing the coin into her left palm she curled her

fingers into a fist around it. Then she held up her fist and slowly opened the fingers to reveal that her hand was completely empty! The coin had vanished.

'How did I do that?' she asked him sassily. 'It's magic! I'm B-Dazzle – and you've been "B-Dazzled"!'

'Badgers' bladders!' breathed Wilf in awe.

'Bravo!' said Jon, putting his hand out. 'Can I have it back now?'

'Sorry, Dad,' said Bel with a perfectly straight face. 'But like you said, lend me a coin and I'll make it disappear, and you'll never see it again!'

Wilfred was shocked. He wouldn't have ever dared to speak to Wincewart like that. But, to Wilfred's astonishment, Jon just laughed, took off Bel's hat and plonked a kiss on her head. Then, turning to Wilf, he grinned and said, 'No wonder I'm broke! How about you, can you do any magic?'

Ye Simple Lighting Spell

Wilfred bowed humbly. 'I am merely a wizard's apprentice, but I do have some basic skills, Lord Dad. May I show thee?' (Honestly? After two disastrous attempts, in two different millennia, Wilf still hadn't learned not to show off his magik?

Maybe Bertram was right calling him Wilfred the 'Unwise'.)

'Go right ahead, and hey, cool banter, Wilf!' said Jon.

Looking around the shop, Wilf's gaze settled on a bright orange spell candle in the display he'd knocked over. 'I shall perform Ye Simple Lighting Spell he announced confidently. Clutching his Bag of Bees magik charm, he muttered the ancient words of the basic spell, adding in a louder voice. 'I command thee to light!'

Everyone looked at the candle. Nothing happened.

Bel looked at Wilfred and pulled a sympathetic face. But to her surprise he was unfazed.

'It does not always light first time!' he shrugged, smiling. He tried again, but this time muttering the spell a little louder and adding, 'Light! I, Wilfred the Wise, command thee.'

Still nothing happened. Bel and Jon exchanged looks.

'Awkward moment,' mouthed Jon to Bel.

Thinking Wilfred must be dying with embarrassment inside, Bel said, 'Wilf, you don't have to do this, you know.'

But Wilfred wasn't at all bothered. 'Sometimes it

takes me a goodly many goes!' he grinned. 'But I can do it! Trust me, I be a wizard!' He laughed.

'She's right. It's not like the sky's going to fall on your head if you can't,' added Jon kindly.

Indeed, Wilfred sincerely hoped that it wouldn't. But he didn't think even he could cause something *that* catastrophic.

Unusually for him, Wilfred was determined not to give up. Taking a deep breath, he focused all his attention on the candle. For the third time, he uttered the incantation and added impressively, 'By the Wondrous White Beard of Wincewart the Withering, I command thee to light!'

The magical spell candle

It might have been that even a twenty-first century spell candle had heard of Wincewart the Withering or, it might just have been third time lucky, *or* it might have been that he was actually concentrating that time, but either way there was a shower of colourful sparks and a puff of turquoise smoke and:

FIZZ, CRACKLE, FLICKER

the candle wick suddenly spluttered into a bright, golden flame.

A broad grin swept over Wilfred's grubby face. (Obviously, it was hard to see under all that muck and grime – but it was there, nonetheless.)

'Neat!' said Bel.

'Awesome!' nodded Jon.

'How did you do it?' demanded Bel.

''Tis but basik magik,' shrugged Wilf modestly.

Bel guessed he must have switched one of Jon's candles with a remote control trick candle when he'd put them back on the shelf, and she just hadn't noticed. But still, it was very impressive – especially the smoke and sparks.

'No, seriously, how do you do the smoke and sparks?' persisted Bel, keen to learn.

'Hey, dudette, you can't expect a magician to give away his secrets!' laughed Jon. Turning to Wilfred he added, 'Can you put it out as well?'

'Verily,' said Wilf and, wisely not pushing his luck with Ye Simple Snuffing Spell, which let's face it, we know he hadn't practised at all, simply blew the candle out. He was rewarded with a burst of laughter and a round of applause. He bowed modestly.

Jon handed him the smoking candle. 'Here, you can have it!'

The only thing Wilfred had ever been given in his entire life was a tatty old pig's bladder football, and that had had a hole in it, so technically it was just a pig's bladder. Wincewart had never given him anything except withering looks, endless tasks and a good many tellings off.

(Oh, and of course three meals a day, a bed, a warm fire and the safety of a hermit cave, all of which was otherwise known as 'a home'.)

'Art thou sure?' asked Wilf.

He'd once used one of Wincewart's prized beeswax spell candles instead of an ordinary, everyday tallow one to light the hermit cave (partly because the stench of burning tallow is disgusting, but mostly because he didn't know the difference). Wincewart had raged on about how expensive spell candles were, and had threatened to turn him into a natterjack toad with smelly feet, foul farts and a very keen sense of smell, if he ever did it again.

'Sure!' shrugged Jon casually, holding out the spell candle.

'Thou art very kind,' replied Wilf humbly, taking it.

'Like it's not yours anyway!' said Bel, thinking Wilf's gratitude was part of his act. 'Anyhow, did you want to look at the crystal balls?'

Remembering the scrying glasses, all so terrifyingly filled with Wincewart's grizzled, angry eyeball, Wilfred flinched. 'I have changed my mind,' he said hurriedly.

A witch in a trinket box!

As they left Crystals and Cauldrons, Bel's phone rang. She hoiked it out of her pocket.

Dung heaps and pigeon poo! What clever sorcery be this now? thought Wilfred, spellbound by the little flat box with its glowing pictures and mysterious symbols. Bel spoke into it. And then he almost fainted. Someone was talking back – from inside the box! (Actually, it was Gloria, asking if they were on their way back.) *A witch in a trinket box!* he marvelled. *And she speaks!*

Wincewart had a witch in a bottle. It was one of his finest possessions, what with it being made out of pretty blue glass, with a silver stopper, *and* having a witch inside it. But it was nowhere near as good as this, because you couldn't actually *talk* to the witch. Come to think of it, there was nothing to prove there really was a witch inside. You just had to take Wincewart's word for it. But this witch was definitely there inside the box.

Chapter Twelve

Hot hounds!

'Can Wilf stay for supper?' Bel asked.

Gloria was closing the cafe for the day, so Bel and Wilf were lugging the tables and chairs in from the pavement.

'Sure!' said Gloria, only too happy that Bel had found someone to hang around with. And anyhow, after catering for what felt like the entire wizarding population of Withering Wallop in the Wold in the cafe all day, feeding one more medium-sized wizard wouldn't make much difference.

Wilfred's face lit up at the thought of food. 'I thank thee, my lady,' he said with a bow.

'Gloria,' corrected Bel's mum with a smile.

'I beg thy pardon, Lady Gloria,' said Wilfred. Gloria laughed and rolled her eyes.

'You've got to admit it – he's good!' grinned Bel, and she realised Wilf hadn't slipped out of character even once all day.

Jon got home just as they were setting the table. He kissed Bel on the top of her head, kissed his wife's cheek and held up his hand for Wilfred to high-five.

Wilf looked at it, baffled.

'Dude! Don't leave me hanging!' joked Jon.

Wilfred put his hand up to copy Jon, and was staggered when Jon casually leant over and slapped it! *Piglets' giblets! He hit me!* thought Wilf, but Jon was carrying on as normal.

'What's for supper?' he was asking.

'Hot dogs!' said Bel.

'Awesome!' cried Jon.

Wilf was horrified. *Hot hounds?* He'd eaten some pretty foul muck in the hermit cave, most of which he'd cooked himself. (Well, if boiling it in a cauldron until it was gloopy counted as cooking). He'd eaten sheep brain broth, calf trotter pottage, hedgehog stew and even actual piglets giblets . . . but dog meat? Never.

He anxiously watched Gloria put two sausages into soft white bread rolls. She handed one to him, and then liberally squirted the other one with a bright red sludge and gave it to Bel.

'Ketchup?' she asked him. Warily, he held out his dog meat and bread, and Gloria plastered it with what looked to Wilfred, very worryingly, like blood.

Tentatively he took a bite . . . and an explosion of delicious spicy meat and tangy tomato erupted into his mouth! 'Zounds! These hot hounds . . . art . . . "awesome"!' he cried, cramming another mouthful in, and then another.

'Thank you!' laughed Gloria. 'Very kind of you to say so.'

'Chef's speciality!' grinned Jon.

'Plenty more,' said Gloria, handing Wilf another one.

Ye Simple Lighting Spell (again)

After supper, Wilfred was amazed when Jon helped to clear the table and load the magik plate washer. He couldn't remember Wincewart ever doing so much as pick up his own platter.

'Wilf, dude, show Gloria that awesome candle-lighting thing you do,' said Jon at the dishwasher.

'Yes!' cried Bel. 'Honest, Mum, it's amazing.'

Wilfred glowed with pride at this high praise from such a mighty enchantress. He gave her his lopsided sheepish grin.

Taking the bright orange candle Jon had given him out of his cloak pocket (or, to be more accurate, Wincewart's cloak pocket) he set it on the table.

He glanced up to see Bel watching him intently. She smiled at him encouragingly.

If my lady Bel believes I can do this, then I must not let her down, he thought.

He focused on the candle, clutched his Bag of Bees, and summoned more concentration than he'd ever previously possessed. As his brow furrowed, his mind cleared of everything except the words for Ye Simple Lighting Spell. He commanded the candle to light.

There was a burst of colourful sparks and a waft of turquoise smoke and, to his relief (not to mention surprise), it lit first time. Jon, Gloria and Bel all burst out clapping.

'Awesome, dude!'

'Brilliant!'

Wilfred bowed modestly. He wasn't used to applause. In fact, he couldn't remember Wincewart ever praising him. But then, to be fair, Wilfred hadn't given the wizard much opportunity to do so.

'You've *so* got to show me how you do that,' grinned Bel.

'Show Wilf some of *your* magic,' said Gloria.

'No,' said Bel flatly.

'Do the spoon bending!' suggested Jon.

'No.'

'Then do the one with the straw wrapper.'

'Again, no!' cried Bel, cringing in embarrassment.

'She's brilliant at that one,' Gloria said to Wilf.

'I'm not going to let you bully me into doing it,' insisted Bel.

'Please, my lady?' begged Wilfred, and he pulled such a funny pleading face, she gave in.

'Oh, all right,' she said and went off to get some paper-wrapped straws from the cafe.

The Astounding Paper-Tearing Trick

A few moments later she came back and sat down at the kitchen table.

'Watch carefully,' she told him as she took the straw out of its wrapper. 'I'm going to tear this ordinary paper wrapper into eight pieces.' She did so and dropped the pieces onto the table. 'And now, I will magic them back together again.' Picking them up she squeezed them into a tight ball, which she put into her hand, and then closed her fist. 'I give it a shake and . . . voila!' She pulled a rolled-up wrapper out of her fist, and unravelled it to show it was now back in one piece.

'Bravo!' cried Jon and Gloria, clapping wildly.

'My lady, thou art indeed a clever enchantress!' laughed Wilf, joining in.

'See, dudette?' said Jon

'We keep telling her that,' said Gloria.

'You're my parents! You would say that, wouldn't you? How can I trust your judgement?' protested Bel.

'Thou can trust *me* – I be a wizard!' said Wilfred earnestly. 'And I think thou art highly skilled!'

Bel smiled at him, went over to the bin and threw the paper away. 'Can we have some pud?' she asked.

'Of course, help yourself,' replied Gloria.

Bel raided the fridge and called out their options. 'Yoghurt? Trifle? Key lime pie?' she asked Wilfred.

'Yes please,' he replied, with absolutely no idea what he was being offered.

'Pig!' said Bel.

'Er, no thank you,' he replied, earnestly shaking his head.

Everyone roared with laughter, so Wilf joined in. He had no idea what he'd said that was funny, but he didn't mind being laughed at. He was getting used to it.

Bel grabbed a handful of puddings and a couple of spoons, and took Wilf upstairs to her bedroom to eat them.

'He seems like a nice lad,' said Gloria to Jon. 'A bit weird, maybe, but nice!'

'He's not weird. He's just into magic. Like me.'

'Yeah, like I said. A bit weird, but nice,' said Gloria, giving him a kiss.

Chapter Thirteen

High wizardry indeed

Nothing, and I mean nothing (well, nothing in all of eleventh century Wallop in the Wold, that is) could have prepared Wilfred for the astounding marvels of Bel's room.

It wasn't just the luxury of the drapes at the windows, or the fact that the windows had *glass* in them, or the size and softness of her bed (far more impressive than Wincewart's) *or* the dark blue woollen tapestry that casually covered the *entire floor*.

It was more the pictures that covered the walls, showing mighty wizards performing spectacular magik. One powerful sorcerer had enchanted a woman to float *in mid-air*. Another had bidden a pack of cards to fly into a hat, and another had sawn a man in half – yet the man was still *alive and smiling*!

'Weasels' warts,' breathed Wilfred. Cautiously, he picked up three large, metal hoops from the top of a wooden chest. 'What be these, my lady?'

'Magic rings,' replied Bel. 'You know, to do the linked hoop trick.'

He didn't know, and begged her to show him.

The Astonishing Ancient Magic Ring Routine

Bel took the hoops, glanced in the mirror to make sure her hat was at the right angle, and began. 'I take three, perfectly ordinary, solid metal hoops,' she said, showing them to Wilfred. 'Watch closely!'

She tossed two of the hoops up in the air and caught them neatly in one hand. To Wilfred's utter amazement when she held them out to show him, the rings were linked together.

'Wizards' gizzards!' he cried, astonished.

She handed the two linked hoops to Wilfred. 'See if you can get them apart.'

Wilfred took one in each hand and pulled. But one ring was linked *inside* the other, and there was no way he could pull them apart. He was astounded.

Bel took them back off him. Then, she rubbed the third hoop against the other rings. 'Shazam!' she cried and suddenly, before Wilfred's very eyes, she held them out like a chain. The three rings were all linked together.

'How did thou do that?' cried Wilf.

'How did I do that?' repeated Bel sassily. 'It's magic! I'm B-Dazzle – and you've been B-Dazzled!'

Wilf was stunned. Melting metal was high magik. Even Wincewart struggled to command metal to do his bidding.

The Amazing Disappearing Card Trick

'Can thou teach me?' he pleaded. If he could learn to do this it would impress the socks off Wincewart when he got back. (Well, it would have done, had the eleventh century wizard actually worn any socks.)

'Sure! But I should warn you it took me months to learn that,' she said.

Wilfred's face fell.

'But I can show you how to make a card disappear. That's much easier,' offered Bel.

Wilf's eyes lit up. Wincewart had been practising Ye Astonishing Disappearing Enchantment for the Midsummer Merrymaking of Magik and Mages all week and, to be honest, it had looked easy enough to Wilfred. But of course it was high magik, and so he wasn't even allowed to attempt it. If Bel could teach him, it would knock his master's sandals off. And also, very possibly, his hat too.

'Watch carefully,' said Bel, holding a card in the palm of her hand. Then she shook the card three times, counting, 'One, two, three!' Then, apparently throwing it into the air, she cried, 'Shazam!' and the card disappeared – right before Wilf's very eyes!

'Let me be thy apprentice!'

Then, seconds later Bel brought the card back again.

Wilfred dropped to his knees.

'I humbly beg thee, my lady, let me be thy apprentice.'

'Idiot!' She laughed. 'Stop larking around! Get up and I'll teach you how to do it!'

Wilfred scrambled to his feet.

'You have to hold the card like this,' said Bel, tucking the card between her fingers.

He took the card eagerly and tried to copy her. But it was harder than it looked and he kept dropping the card, or bending it so that it flipped out of his hand. He tried a few times, but just couldn't seem to grasp it. 'Dragons' armpits!' he laughed. 'I be hopeless! I cannot do it!'

'It's a knack,' shrugged Bel. 'Took me a while to do it right.'

'Be I doing it wrong?' he asked, as the card slipped out of his fingers for the umpteenth time.

'No, you've just got to keep practising.'

So Wilfred tried a few more times, but he still couldn't do it.

'I give up,' he grinned, rolling his eyes.

So, very patiently, Bel started to show him again. But Wilf could clearly remember that when Wincewart did Ye Astonishing Disappearing Enchantment back in the cave, it didn't seem to be anywhere near as tricky as Bel's method.

Some chalk and a pentacle

So he suddenly announced, 'My lady, I do not need to learn this way. I can do the magik by another method. Would thou have some chalk?'

'Er, yes,' said Bel, getting him a piece out of her desk drawer.

'I thank thee,' said Wilfred, grinning. Then, in an attempt to copy her banter, he stood in the middle of the room and said, 'Thou must watch closely. I be Wilfred the Wise, and thou art about to be . . . er . . .'

'B-Dazzled?' grinned Bel.

'Bedazzled' agreed Wilf earnestly.

With a confident flourish, Wilfred enchanted his new spell candle to light. Then, he chalked a pentacle on the dark blue carpet and stepped into the centre. Flamboyantly holding out the playing card in one hand, and clutching his Bag of Bees charm in the other, he muttered the incantation for Ye Astonishing Disappearing Enchantment. Or rather, what he *thought* was the incantation.

'Heed ye words of mine enchantment,
O strange-small-paper-card-with-curious-symbols-
written-upon-thee.

Thou must vanish!
I do banish
thee from sight.'

There was a blinding flash, a torrent of brightly coloured sparks and a loud

KA-BOOM!

And a huge cloud of turquoise smoke billowed into the room.

'Witches' wrinkles!' screamed Wilfred, frantically wafting smoke away from him and up to the ceiling . . . and promptly setting off the fire alarm.

DRIIIII-IIIING!

It was painfully and terrifyingly deafening, and Wilfred screamed.

'Aaaaaaaargh!'

'Uh oh!' said Bel calmly.

Messed-up magik and mayhem

Jon and Gloria pounded up the stairs.

'Bel! Are you all right?' yelled her mum, charging in.

'Where's the fire?' cried Jon.

'Everything's fine,' shouted Bel over the screaming alarm, and, casually climbing on her bed, she reached up and turned it off. Clouds of turquoise smoke hung around the room. Wilfred hung behind Bel.

'Where's all this smoke come from?' asked Gloria, shoving the bedroom window open.

Wilfred peered anxiously out around Bel. 'My noble lady, I be truly sorry,' he said. 'A small enchantment did not go to plan,' he finished sheepishly.

'It was lucky you didn't set the sprinklers off!' said Gloria. 'Be more careful!'

'But hey, no harm done, dude,' said Jon to Wilfred, who grinned sheepishly.

Her mum and dad went back downstairs and Bel grimaced at Wilfred.

'I think maybe you'd better go.'

Her parents were usually pretty chilled, but Bel didn't dare risk setting off the sprinklers and drenching the entire cafe. It'd be a disaster if they had to close during the festival week to let everything dry out.

Wilf nodded sadly. He guessed she wouldn't want him as an apprentice now. He wasn't really surprised. But he brightened up when she held out the pack of cards. 'Do you want to borrow these?'

'Art thou sure?'

'Absolutely. You need the practice!' she laughed, and Wilfred grinned at her.

'It was awesome, by the way, all that smoke and the sparks. But next time, you might want to try to make the card disappear as well. Since that's the point!' she added sarcastically.

Wilfred nodded earnestly. 'I will try, my lady.' Then added hopefully, 'Dost this mean I *can* be thy apprentice? Not for ever –' since he was still apprenticed to Wincewart – 'but just while I be here?'

'Sure – whatever! But you have to promise to show me how you do the sparks and smoke thing.' That would certainly make her act stand out from all the rest, she thought. Not to mention making it drop-dead awesome and, well, B-Dazzling!

'I promise, my lady!' cried Wilfred, grinning broadly and swearing to himself he'd become a better apprentice than he had been. 'I thank thee mightily. I will work hard and thou will not regret it!' (If Wincewart had heard this, he would have bet his hat, two spell candles and his lucky rabbit's foot on a leather thong that she would.)

The enchanted tent

'Where are you staying?' asked Bel.

'If I be thy apprentice, can I not stay here?'

'But what about your family? Won't they wonder where you are?'

'I have no family, my lady. I was left at the wall of my Lord Wallop's castle many moons ago.' (Many thousands of moons ago, actually. Twelve thousand, is it? Oh, I don't know. You do the sums.) 'Wincewart found me and took me in and I have been with him ever since.'

'So where is he now?'

Wilfred realised he didn't know where his master was *precisely*, so he said, 'I be not sure.'

'Well, is he in Withering Wallop in the Wold?'

'Verily!'

'Where did you see him last?'

Wilfred thought back. 'He was heading to the castle.'

'So is he taking part in the festival?'

'My lady, he is performing the finale,' he said proudly.

'In that case I bet he's at the castle campsite! Has he got a tent?'

'No.'

Bel knelt down, reached under her bed and hauled out her pop-up tent. Shoving it at Wilfred, she said: 'Here. It's dead easy to put up.'

'Be it enchanted then?' he asked.

'No! You just pull this tag and . . .' But before she could stop him, Wilf did exactly that and:

FLUUUMPH!

'Aaaaaargh!' he screamed, as the tent exploded open, trapping him against the wall. 'Battered beetles!' he cried. 'It has attacked me! Help!'

Chapter Fourteen

Bertram be a poor apprentice

By suppertime both Bertram and Wincewart were in extraordinarily foul tempers. Bertram was livid that he'd been expected to spend hours slaving away at a seemingly endless list of household chores – as if he were a mere apprentice!

And Wincewart was irritated beyond measure when Bertram had proved to be spectacularly useless at them.

For a start, the bird couldn't gather wood. 'I do

not have hands!' he had squawked witheringly. 'I cannot carry kindling.'

And he couldn't light the lamps. 'I have feathers, not fingers! I cannot strike the tinder box!'

And he didn't even try to carry the water bucket. 'It be far too big for mine claws, Wincewart!' he had squawked.

'Then try with thy beak! Thou has a big enough beak for anything!' snapped the wizard. 'AND DO NOT CALL ME WINCEWART!'

Bertram ruffled his feathers pointedly. He had worked his wings to the bone, broken a feather, and had even had to muck out his own bird poo. And he'd not had a word of thanks from the wizard.

'What be for supper?' snapped Wincewart, adding insult to injury.

'There be something stewing in the pot,' retorted his familiar peevishly.

The wizard peered into the huge cauldron simmering on the fire, and stared first with suspicion and then with horror at the grey gruel inside. Cautiously he ladled up a spoonful and dribbled it sloppily into a bowl. It looked disgusting. He wished Wilfred were back. Even *his* cooking was better than this.

Wincewart brooded darkly for a while then suddenly turned to his familiar and announced, 'If the boy be not back by tomorrow I will get another apprentice.'

Wincewart's apprentices

Bertram cast his mind back over Wincewart's previous apprentices.

Wilbert the Wilful, Wolfgang the Workshy, Worrell the Wretched, Witlock the Witless, Wolcot the Worthless and Wrybald the Wretched.

They'd been a pretty dire bunch of snotty-nosed peasant boys who, with their scruffy hair and filthy faces, had all looked pretty much the same to Bertram. And none of them – *none* of them – had treated the raven with the respect he deserved as familiar to the most powerful wizard in all of Wallop in the Wold.

And worse, as soon as any of them learnt to do the simplest bit of basik magik, they got cocky and started to look down on him as if he were a mere raven.

Bertram sighed. He was undoubtedly smarter than the lot of them – he could actually read the entire

Ye Ancient Yet Complete Runic Record of Magik Charms and Enchantments, for a start. Frankly, he'd have preferred it if Wincewart didn't have an apprentice *at all*.

Except that, as he was now only too aware, not only did he hate doing chores, there was a painfully long list of things to get ready for the Midsummer Merrymaking of Magik and Mages as well. He eyed the parchment where it lay on the table, its corners and edges weighted down with crystals and charm stones to stop it rolling back up again. It was very long – almost as long as the table. So he fluttered over to Wincewart, and suggested they draw up a list of village lads he could take on as a new apprentice. Preferably one that couldn't whistle.

It was a surprisingly short list.

A shortlist of three

You might imagine that a lot of boys would have given their eyeteeth to become an apprentice wizard in ye olden days when magic was . . . actually, to be honest I'm not sure how to put this . . . so I'm going with 'real'. But in truth there were better career options, even in eleventh century Wallop in the Wold.

Obviously none of the castle pages would give up the chance of becoming a knight, and none of the farm lads would want to be cooped up indoors all day. Even the lowliest castle servant, the scullion boy, wouldn't swap the comforts of a full belly and a warm kitchen for a meagre diet of wrinkled mangel-wurzels, limp nettles, dry bread and flat, dusty ale, as well as the cold floor of a hermit cave for a bed.

And of course a girl was *completely* out of the question.

So they came up with a shortlist of three. Oswald, the cobbler's lad, Ludgar the Pigboy, and Perkin, the son of the gong farmer (or Perkin the Pongy as he was more commonly known).

'Which one be the cleverest?' Wincewart wisely asked. He was sitting in his huge, ornate chair with his elbows on the oak table, tapping his fingertips together thoughtfully in front of the scorched remains of his beard.

'Oswald, the cobbler's lad. He has a quick brain and quicker fingers,' replied Bertram.

'Then methinks I shall take him.'

'Art thou sure?'

'Verily. Trust me, I be a wizard,' replied Wincewart pompously.

'But he be the castle sneak thief,' squawked Bertram, with his head on one side.

'Ah,' said Wincewart, thinking about his valuable wizarding equipment and enchantment ingredients. 'Then perchance not him.' Wilfred, to his certain knowledge, had never stolen so much as a slice of rye bread. 'What about Ludgar the Pigboy? Be he clever?'

'Not as clever as the pig,' cawed Bertram.

For all his faults, Wincewart had to admit that even Wilfred was brighter than the average hog. Well, just about.

'Ah, in that case, methinks not him either,' said Wincewart.

'But that leaves Perkin. Perkin the Pongy! The son of the gong farmer – the poo-man! Thou cannot be serious! He stinks to high heaven!' Bertram protested, flapping his wings in horror. 'He makes the sheep retch and the wood pigeons faint – even the bluebottles won't land on him!'

The wizened wizard grimaced and his pointed nose wrinkled uncontrollably. Wincewart began to think that against this motley mob, even Wilfred might be the best bet. Even *with* the whistling.

So he said, 'Let us not be hasty. And anyhow, methinks Wilfred will be back soon.'

Where has that turnip-head gone?

For the umpteenth time that evening the mighty wizard strode to the mouth of the cave, his robe billowing majestically, and peered out at the darkening hillside in the hope of seeing Wilfred sidling back, embarrassed and full of apology.

And not *just* because the other options for an apprentice were all so downright dreadful. Wincewart was surprised to find how much he missed Wilfred's cheerfulness, his lopsided sheepish grin and even his tuneless and irritating whistling. Despite despairing of him on a daily basis, the wizard was fond of him. Very fond of him, in fact. Though he would never have admitted it, even if you'd threatened to shave off the remains of his precious beard with a blunt and rusty knife.

'Where has that lumpen, doltish, turnip-head gone?' he grumbled. 'I was sure he would be back when night fell.'

'I was sure he would be back when his belly was empty,' cawed his familiar.

Wincewart was beginning to get anxious. It wasn't exactly safe to be out after dark in eleventh century Wallop in the Wold. It was well known that fierce, fiery dragons and ravenous wolves roamed around, wild and dangerous. And Wilfred was only a boy. Wincewart shuddered. 'Thou do not think something terrible has happened to him?' he asked Bertram.

'Thou art not that lucky,' replied the raven sarcastically.

Chapter Fifteen

The magical campsite

Bel and Wilfred got to the castle, and found the festival campsite was already a sea of tents. Bel looked around, hoping to find a space.

Wilf looked around, taking it all in. It was truly magikal. Lights and lanterns hung on the tents and in the trees, and colourful flags and magik charms fluttered from tent poles. Wind chimes tinkled in the breeze, and campfires and barbecues glowed invitingly all around. Laughing children and barking dogs ran around excitedly, and there were more wizards, witches and druids than you could shake a sorcerer's staff at.

'Will Wincewart be able to find you amongst this lot?' asked Bel.

Wilfred shrugged.

'Does he have a phone?'

'Um . . .' replied Wilfred vaguely, not knowing what a 'phone' was.

'I take that as a no,' said Bel. *All very hippy dippy*, she thought, *but not very responsible.*

But she was reassured when Wilf waved cheerfully to a family nearby, who waved back. Sighing happily, he said, 'It be just like home!'

Well, he seems to know these people, thought Bel, reassured.

So they found a space in the far corner, near the road, and Bel got out the tent. Wilfred stood well back.

As well as her sleeping bag, Bel had bunged a few 'essential items' into a rucksack for Wilf: a box of juice, a packet of biscuits, some crisps, a chocolate bar and her wind-up torch.

Wilfred was instantly entranced by the torch. He was like a toddler with a new toy, endlessly switching it on and off, amazed that he could command it to light and snuff, over and over again, and without any enchantment at all.

Finally, Bel had to take it off him. And now he was whistling cheerfully, if tunelessly, and busily building a small campfire. Actually, much to her alarm, he was building rather a large one.

'Um, I think that's probably enough wood,' she said, anxiously looking around at the other tents, which weren't exactly a million miles away.

Wilfred disagreed. 'But I need a mighty blaze to fend off wolves and dragons.'

'Actually, we don't get a lot of dragons around here. Or wolves,' she said flatly. 'In fact, I can't remember the last time I saw one.'

Neither could Wilfred, but that didn't stop him hurling another armful of wood onto the pile. Bel consoled herself with the thought that he didn't have any matches.

He didn't. But he did have eleventh century magik. So Wilfred crouched down, pointed at the pile of dry wood, and, clutching his Bag of Bees, commandingly muttered Ye Simple Lighting Spell.

It took him a couple of goes, but suddenly there was an impressive shower of sparks and a puff of turquoise smoke, and a small flame flickered in the centre of the woodpile. He blew on it to fan it to a roaring blaze.

Magic – not science

'How did you do that?' demanded Bel, gobsmacked. She was sure he hadn't had time to set anything up like he had with the candle in the shop. So how had he done it?

Wilfred shrugged modestly.

'No, seriously,' said Bel. 'You just a started fire out of *nothing*!'

'It be not as clever as this!' declared Wilfred, switching the torch on and off again, delightedly. 'This be crafty sorcery indeed!'

'No,' said Bel, taking the torch off him again. '*This* is science. But *that*,' she said, indicating the roaring fire, '*that* was . . . was . . .' There was no other word for it. 'That was *magic*!' For the second time that day, Bel had been bedazzled by something Wilfred had done, and wasn't entirely sure what she'd seen.

The dark had crept up surprisingly quickly, and a full yellow moon hung heavy and low behind the dark branches of the trees. (You know, the sort of moons wolves howl at. Well, they would if there were actually any around in twenty-first century Withering Wallop in the Wold.)

'I'd better get home. Will you be all right?' asked Bel, suddenly anxious again about leaving him on his own. (He was hardly 'alone' – there were dozens of families nearby, but you know what she meant.)

'Yes, my lady!' grinned Wilfred, 'I shall practise my spells.'

'Okay. Well, night then,' said Bel, turning and walking off.

Wilfred watched her go, and suddenly felt lonely. She was his only friend in this new time, and although he was surrounded by people, they were all strangers. But, looking on the bright side, she'd be back tomorrow. He only had to get through the night . . . the long, dark night with all its perils and dangers. Anxiously he flung another great stack of wood on the fire – just to be on the safe side.

As Bel walked home, a small but hugely improbable thought flickered and then grew in her mind. Maybe Wilf really was an apprentice wizard from the eleventh century? Otherwise, how else could he *literally* magic fire from nothing?

If he's not a genuine eleventh-century wizard's

apprentice, then he's doing a pretty convincing job of pretending that he is, she thought.

Bel had studied a lot of magicians, and she knew exactly how they did a lot of their tricks . . . but she'd never seen anyone do what Wilf had just done.

Oh, don't be ridiculous, she told herself. *There's no such thing as real magic . . .* But she couldn't quite shake the niggle from her mind that, well, that there was, and that she'd literally just witnessed some in action.

Dragonflies' farts!

Back at the camp, Wilf had taken out Bel's pack of cards and was preparing to practise Ye Astonishing Disappearing Enchantment. He chalked a pentacle onto the grass, stepped into it, and under the light of the moon he clutched his Bag of Bees and muttered the ancient incantation – well, as best as he could remember it.

It all looked very magical, and mysterious and utterly convincing. It was just a shame it didn't work.

Which, given his spectacular failure in Bel's

bedroom, probably doesn't surprise you. It didn't particularly surprise Wilfred either. But what *might* surprise you is that, unusually for him, he didn't give up.

But then, for the first time in his life, Wilfred could see *the point* of not giving up. All the wizards in his own time were ancient, wrinkled and wizened: white-haired old men who swore it took decades to learn the mystical arts of sorcery. No one expected, or even allowed, a mere boy to do anything other than the most basik magik for *years*.

But here (or was it now?) sorcerers as young as him could perform the most *spectacular* high magik. Wilfred reckoned that if he worked hard, and learnt as much as he could from Bel, then he would indeed become a powerful wizard. And not after years and years – but soon! So he decided to keep trying to remember Ye Astonishing Disappearing Enchantment until he got it right.

After about a hundred hopeless attempts, a dense pall of turquoise smoke hung around Wilfred and he'd produced more colourful sparks than a fully-grown dragon with hiccups. But at last, to his utter joy, he stumbled on the right words – entirely by good luck (well, good luck and persistence, to be fair) – and finally he managed to get a card to disappear.

'Dragonflies' farts! I have done it!' he cried, and leapt into the air joyfully. Then he sat back down eagerly to do it again . . . and again . . . and again.

He had made a good many cards vanish before he realised that, unlike Bel, he couldn't actually get them to reappear. They were disappearing for good.

Maybugs' belches!

So he tried using Ye Spectacular Summoning Charm to get the next card from the pack to fly into his hand, making it look as though the card had returned. Of course it wasn't *exactly* what Bel had done – but it looked impressive nonetheless.

And, he noticed, he was definitely getting better at that spell too. There was hardly any smoke and just a sprinkle of tiny red-hot sparks, so only a couple of cards had actually burst into flames. Most were only very slightly singed round the edges. *They be hardly burned at all, really,* he told himself. He wished Wincewart were there to see him.

Sighing contentedly, he took the cheese and onion crisps from the rucksack and tore it open. This time last night (or this time a millennium ago, if you prefer) he'd been scrubbing and boiling soggy mangel-wurzels for supper in a gloomy cave under the sharp eye of Wincewart and the sharper tongue of Bertram the Raven.

Maybugs' belches, I like this new time, he thought, crunching away. *I like it a lot.*

He was startled when a voice said, 'Excuse me, lad,' and he looked up to see an elderly wizard looming over him.

Chapter Sixteen

Marvin the Marvellous, Morgana and Faye

The wizard wore a long, dark robe, and a short white beard. Two very young witches stood next to him, their faces painted with silver cobwebs and black spiders. The effect was magikal, and Wilf was entranced.

'Sorry to bother you, lad, but I can't get my barbecue going,' the wizard continued. 'I see you've got a good fire there. Wondered if you could give me a hand?'

Wilfred hadn't a clue what a barbecue was, but he was more than happy to help, and he cheerfully followed them over to their tent. A small metal tray of coals sat on the ground outside, smoking feebly. Wilfred immediately grasped the problem and, kneeling down, quickly (and magikally) set it alight. A small waft of turquoise smoke drifted above the flames.

'Wow!' said the elderly wizard. 'That was impressive!

'I thank thee,' said Wilfred with a modest bow.

'Kids, whack those burgers on,' said the wizard. Slapping Wilfred on the shoulder he added, 'Sit yourself down and have a burger with us!'

Wilfred didn't need to ask what a burger was, any more than he needed to be asked more than once if he wanted one. The girls were already plonking round slabs of meat onto flames. Wilfred sat on the ground and the old wizard struggled to sit down next to him, complaining about his creaky knees as he did so. He reminded Wilfred of Wincewart, only much younger.

Wilfred suddenly remembered his manners. 'I be Wilfred the Wise,' he said, bowing politely.

'Wilfred the Wise, eh? Mind if I call you Wilf? I'm Marvin the Marvellous – but you can call me Marv. That's Morgana and that's Faye,' he said, indicating which of the girls was which. (Or rather, which of the girls was which witch.)

Flaming marshmallows!

Despite already having eaten several hot dogs, three puddings and a packet of crisps, Wilfred still managed to polish off a couple of burgers, both heavily smothered with ketchup.

And then Faye and Morgana showed him how to toast marshmallows. They couldn't believe Wilf had never done it before. But after he'd burnt the first ones to a cinder, and let the next ones melt completely and drop off his stick, and then set fire to the stick itself, they could well believe it.

'Here, let me do it,' said Morgana, quickly stuffing two marshmallows onto a stick for him and skilfully toasting them to perfection.

'It's a knack,' Faye explained. 'You have to get them near enough to the flames so they go brown on the outside, and gloopy in the middle.'

Morgana handed the cooked marshmallows to Wilfred. 'There you go,' she said.

'Careful, they're HOT!' warned Faye, just as he was about to shove them straight into his mouth.

'Blow on them,' said Morgana. 'And then just take a small bite.'

Cautiously Wilfred did so . . . and couldn't believe the heavenly, light, melting sweetness on his tongue. 'Hmmmmm,' he mumbled ecstatically, and suddenly wished Wincewart was there to try them. 'May I take a marshmallow with me?' he asked Marv.

'Of course! Here, take a handful!' said the wizard, holding open the packet.

Wilfred took two marshmallows and put them carefully in his pocket. He would cook them for Wincewart when he got back to his own time.

Then he grabbed another handful and crammed them onto his toasting stick.

'Steady on!' laughed Marv.

Eagerly Wilfred held the marshmallows over the flames. But by now the small barbecue was dying down so, clutching his Bag of Bees, he pointed at the marshmallows and impatiently muttered Ye Simple Lighting Spell.

WOOOOMPH!

All his marshmallows immediately burst into flames, and Wilfred found himself holding a huge, blazing torch! 'Help!' he cried, waggling it furiously to try to put out the flames.

'Stop waving it about! You'll set the tent on fire!' cried Marv. 'Drop it on the ground!'

Wilfred did so and Marv instantly stamped on the blazing marshmallows and put the flames out.

'I do be sorry,' said Wilfred humbly. 'I be a clumsy oaf!'

'Never mind, lad. But I think it's probably time to go to bed,' said Marv, scraping the sticky goo off the soles of his walking boots and onto the grass.

Wilfred stood up to leave.

'Thanks for your help, Wilf,' said Marv.

Wilfred grinned and bowed, 'Nay, I thank thee for mine supper!'

'Night, Wilf,' chorused the girls, going into their tent.

'I bid thee goodnight,' replied Wilfred.

'Sleep tight, mind the bugs don't bite!' laughed Marv.

Which sent Wilfred heading back to his tent, remembering the bed bugs back in the cave and scratching furiously.

The Simple Card Levitation Trick

Standing in her PJs in front of her bedroom mirror, Bel was skilfully practising a card levitation trick. It was a simple illusion (relying on a small strip of plastic stuck on the back of the card) where you made the card look like it was floating above your hand.

Frankly, Bel had mastered it years ago. The problem was that it *looked* simple and like anyone could do it. Bel didn't want to do the same old tricks everyone else could do. She liked to add a spin to them to make them her own. Or, better still, invent something completely new that left people wondering exactly how they'd been B-Dazzled.

'It's boring,' she told herself critically. 'You need to snazz it up. Maybe with a few flashing sparks or some coloured smoke like Wilf does.'

And, for the umpteenth time, she wondered how he did it. He'd said he'd teach her, but Bel was impatient. Not in the same way as Wilfred, who wanted to be able to do everything immediately without any practice. When Bel saw a new trick she wanted to start *learning* it immediately. And, since she was entirely self-taught, she wasn't used to having to sit around waiting and twiddling her thumbs.

Putting the card back in its pack, she stored it neatly away in her chest of drawers, the one labelled 'PLAYING CARDS and PAPER PROPS'. She'd banished all her clothes to her wardrobe so she had somewhere to keep her magic stuff.

To be honest, she didn't have a great many props (nowhere near as many as she wanted) and most of them could have been crammed into the bottom drawer, or a box under her bed. But Bel was meticulous about the tools of her trade, whereas she couldn't care less about clothes.

Being able to lay her hands on the right deck of cards for the Disappearing Trick, or the precise length of rope for the Vanishing Knot, or the five-pound note she used in the Folding Fiver illusion, was much more important than being able to find a clean pair of knickers or matching socks, any day.

Smoke and sparks

She picked up her tablet, sat cross-legged on her bed, and searched 'MAGIC TRICKS + SPARKS'. Lots of sites showed you how to make sparks by snapping your fingers and thumbs, either by cheating with a laser light or making real sparks by using a couple of powders that exploded when you put them together. But the chemicals were so dangerous you had to keep them in separate containers, and only use a tiny amount each time.

Mum'd have a fit if I tried that! she thought, with a horrifying but spectacular vision of blowing up the entire Enchanted Cave Cafe. But nothing showed her how to make a dazzling display of sparks in thin air like Wilf could.

So she had a quick search for smoke effects, but she'd looked it up before and knew you needed either a really expensive bit of kit or, guess what, some more dangerous chemicals. And anyhow, these only made a few small wisps of ordinary smoke – nothing like the clouds of multicoloured stuff Wilf could conjure. Bel sighed. She'd just have to wait.

She thought about him lighting the candle in the shop. She was pretty certain the 'spell candle' was just an ordinary remote control candle. But what about at the campfire? He couldn't have put his 'spell candle' in amongst the wood. She'd have seen it. It was bright orange, for crying out loud! And anyhow, would he really sacrifice a remote control candle just to pretend he could magically light a bonfire? They weren't exactly cheap . . . So how had he done that?

Thinking about him, and his act as 'Wilfred the Wise', she realised it was actually very clever. On the one hand, decked out like a wizard's apprentice from the olden days, he pretended to be completely baffled by anything modern. But on the other hand, he relied on state-of-the-art magic devices to do his special effects.

That's smart, she thought. You'd expect a modern magician to use technology. But Wilf's medieval costume and banter lulled the audience into thinking he wouldn't – which made what he did all the more unexpected.

Maybe she should ditch her cool, contemporary B-Dazzle persona, with her stripy top, leggings and pork-pie hat, and go for something 'olde worlde' instead? *Nah*, she thought. *It just wouldn't be me.*

It was late, so she slid under the duvet and snuggled down. Suddenly she remembered Wilf, all alone at the campsite. She hoped he'd be all right, and immediately decided to get up dead early and make sure.

So she set the alarm on her phone for 6 a.m.,

plugged it in to charge overnight, and then put it on her bedside table.

Then a few moments later she sat up and re-set the alarm for 5.30 a.m.

Dragons!

A scruff of brown hair stuck out of the top of Bel's sleeping bag. Snuggled down inside, Wilfred was deep in a dreamless sleep. It was nearly midnight and he was dead-beat. (Well, a thousand years is a long way to travel in a single day.)

But he was suddenly aware of a low grumbling, throaty roar, growing louder and louder. Wrenching himself awake, he shot upright, his heart thudding in fear. Fumbling with the tent zip, he peered out. The deafening roar was closer – almost upon him! Suddenly he saw streaks of hot white light tearing along the road towards him. Then the lights flickered white and red like flames . . . and a steady stream of huge motorbikes thundered by.

VERRROOOOOOM!

'DRAGONS!' screamed Wilfred, 'DRAGONS!' Frantically he pelted from tent to tent waking everyone up, bellowing, 'Dragons! Save thy selves!'

Panic-stricken campers in pyjamas and bare feet stumbled around in the dark, tripping over tent pegs and swearing. Half a dozen dogs charged about yelping and snapping at anyone in reach. Bright torchlights swept the campsite like searchlights, and everyone was yelling at everyone else and demanding to know what was going on.

When they finally calmed down enough to discover that the cause of the commotion was a young lad dressed up as a wizard and swearing blind he'd seen a clan of hideous, fire-breathing dragons, they were, understandably, furious.

A group of particularly angry campers told Wilfred exactly what they would do to him, *and just how much it would hurt,* if he so much as dared to wake them up again. Wilfred was quaking in his eleventh-century boots until Marv stepped in.

'Come on, folks, he's just a lad. He's probably just had a bit of a nightmare. No harm done,' then turning to Wilfred, Marv added, 'I think you'd best slope off back to your tent!'

Wolf!

Miserably, Wilfred crept back to his tent and grabbed the sleeping bag. Then he wrapped it around him and squatted by the fire, on guard, too scared to go back to sleep. In the distance a farm dog howled hauntingly. (You know, like a hungry wolf.)

HOO-OOWL

'Maggots' mumps! He sounds starving!' Wilfred shivered. *I like not this new time. I like it not at all! I wish Wincewart were here*, he thought.

Nervously scanning the shadows for a glimpse of a prowling, ravening wolf, Wilfred piled wood onto his fire and fanned the flames. Then he tried whistling cheerfully to keep his spirits up until –

'STOP THAT WHISTLING!' yelled an angry voice.

So, wisely, he did.

Chapter Seventeen

Wincewart's dream

Back in ye olde hermit cave, Wincewart had slept poorly. He'd tossed and turned all night on his sheepskin bed, wracked with bad dreams, one of which had been horribly vivid.

He'd dreamt he was performing at the Midsummer Merrymaking of Magik and Mages – but everything was going horribly wrong. Spell candles melted, incantations came out as gibberish, and his cauldron sprouted legs and ran away.

Peasants pointed at him, sniggering and heckling,

while Wilfred sat high on the battlements, wearing Wincewart's best cloak and tauntingly dangling his silver dragon's claw talisman.

And worse, looking down, Wincewart saw that although he was trying to make himself disappear, he had only succeeded in making *his clothes* vanish. He was as naked as a new-born babe, except for his boots!

He begged Wilfred to let him have his cloak back, but Wilfred was being swept away by a hoard of fire-breathing dragons!

No wonder Wincewart woke in a cold sweat.

Still Wilfred has not returned

As he lay in his bed, and the early morning summer sun did its best to brighten all the nooks and crannies of the hermit cave, it was immediately obvious to Wincewart that Wilfred had not returned.

There was no cheerful, tuneless and frankly irritating whistling for a start, and no breakfast on the go. It was also obvious to the wizard that Bertram the Beady, hunched on his perch with his beak tucked under one wing, was still asleep.

Wincewart threw his boot at his perch. It was a good shot. The pole wobbled wildly and the bird woke up.

'The boy be not back,' announced Wincewart baldly.

Bertram's heart sank, realising a full day's work would lie ahead of him, starting with getting the wizard's breakfast.

While Bertram busied himself at the cauldron, Wincewart sat at the table, stroking the scorched remains of his beard thoughtfully.

'Perchance I was too harsh on him,' he said. 'Methinks he did not mean to lose mine talisman. He be good and honest at heart and cannot help being a dunderhead and a dolt. I was sure he would return by the morn. I be worried about him.'

'Methinks Wilfred has found a new, richer master,' announced the raven, glumly fluttering over to perch on the wizard's shoulder.

'What?' spluttered the wizard.

'I have been thinking on it. Did thou not see with thy own eyes a cavern filled with priceless magikal goods?'

Indeed Wincewart had (when he'd spied the inside of Jon's shop through his scrying glass).

'Perhaps he has deserted thee for a more successful master?' squawked Bertram.

'Great talismans of trickery!' roared Wincewart, leaping up so suddenly that Bertram fell off. 'He would not be so bold and saucy as to get another master.'

'Yet I think he has,' observed his familiar. 'And more, I wonder if he has taken thy talisman with him?'

There was a dramatic pause, then an even more dramatic outburst.

'He would not dare! HE WOULD NOT DARE!' thundered Wincewart, clutching his cloak where the dragon's claw clasp should have been. 'The talisman will be here in the cave somewhere! IT MUST BE!' he bellowed. 'RAVEN! We shall search in all the chests and cauldrons, hunt through all the charms and potions, explore every nook and cranny, and we shall not stop until we find it!'

'Oh, joy be mine, more work,' muttered Bertram sarcastically under his breath.

Wincewart the Worried

Wincewart sat in his chair, brusquely ordering Bertram about, as the poor raven poked around

the pantry shelf, peered in all the cauldrons and rummaged through the star charts, enchanted quill pens and coloured spell candles.

When that failed, Wincewart commanded his familiar to search every single one of the pots of magikal potions and each and every one of the boxes of charm stones, spell bones and crystals.

But still they did not find the talisman.

Feverish and increasingly angry, Wincewart up-ended all the boxes and chests and stores, until chalices and amulets and all manner of magikal paraphernalia littered the floor, and the huge oak table was cluttered with enchantment ingredients.

The wizard even drained the flagon of ale from the pantry shelf. Partly to see if the talisman was inside, but mostly because he needed a drink to steady his nerves.

Suddenly Wincewart slapped his hand against his furrowed brow, and said, 'Sorcerers' sores! I be an idiot! I can use Ye Ancient Seeing Spell to look for the talisman! Why did I not think of that before?'

'That be a good question,' Bertram cawed dryly, eyeing the chaos in the cave. If a raven had eyebrows, he would have lifted one witheringly.

Wincewart the Angry

The ancient wizard grasped his scrying glass to his lap, and eagerly intoned Ye Ancient Seeing Spell:

> '*Oh, crystal ball*
> *Thou can see all.*
> *I command thee,*
> *Reveal to me . . .*
> *Where my most-prized-and-priceless-solid-silver-dragon's-claw-talisman-of-potency do be.*'

Swirls of deep blue smoke filled the glass and then cleared to reveal . . . flames. Nothing but flames.

Looking over his shoulder into the sphere Bertram said, 'Did thou do the spell wrong?'

'No!'

'Art thou sure?'

'Yes!'

'Thou must have done!' persisted Bertram.

'I DID NOT!' thundered Wincewart.

'Then why can thou only see flames?'

Wincewart's dreadful dream came back to him.

He gasped out loud. 'Methinks it was stolen by a hoard of terrifying fire-breathing dragons who swept poor Wilfred away with them!'

Logically, if somewhat scathingly, Bertram pointed out there was no sign whatsoever of a hoard of terrifying fire-breathing dragons having been in the cave. And, since eleventh century dragons were renowned for leaving a lot of clues like scorch marks on the walls, and most of your furniture burnt to cinders, Wincewart had to agree with him.

'But where be my talisman?' groaned Wincewart.

(Now, I *could* tell you where the talisman is – but that would be a bit of a spoiler, wouldn't it? But I will tell you that it's still in the hermit cave and that if you were playing 'hunt the thimble for it', and you actually found it, then you'd be very hot indeed.)

'Methinks it was stolen by Wilfred,' announced Bertram glumly.

The ancient wizard turned a dangerous shade of deep purple. 'By the cauldron of Crispin the Crafty! When I get my hands on that ungrateful, churlish, lumpen, light-fingered, thieving, dung beetle of a boy I will –!' He stopped, temporarily speechless, then spluttered, 'Never speak his name to me again!'

And thrusting his scrying glass into its wooden case with such force he all but broke it, he slammed the lid shut so loudly, the sound echoed round the cave.

Chapter Eighteen

A dragon's scale

Bel arrived at the campsite at dawn, with a carton of chocolate milkshake and a cold ham and pineapple pizza for Wilf.

She wasn't surprised to find everyone still asleep and the tents zipped closed. But she *was* surprised to see Wilf squatting forlornly outside the tent, wrapped in her sleeping bag, looking like he'd been awake all night.

'Wilf, are you OK?'

'My lady, no! I be not!'

'Why? What happened?!' she asked anxiously.

Wilfred took a deep breath and began, 'There were many dragons roaring and breathing fire . . .'

'Dragons,' cut in Bel flatly.

Wilfred nodded earnestly. 'And they woke this ravenous wolf –'

'Wolf,' repeated Bel witheringly, and unintentionally sounding quite a lot like Wincewart.

'Yes, and it howled with hunger all night. I cannot sleep here again,' he announced, worriedly running his hand through his hair. 'It be not safe!'

'O-kay,' said Bel, thinking Wilf had either let his imagination run riot with him or that he must have had some pretty vivid nightmares. She handed him the shake and the pizza, and he tucked in heartily.

Hasn't hit his appetite, she observed as she stuffed the sleeping bag in the rucksack and collapsed the tent. Then she slung the bag over her shoulder and left him to carry the tent.

Wilfred wanted to say his farewells to Marvin the Marvellous, Faye and Morgana, but their tent was still shut. So he and Bel headed back home along the road.

'Look!' he cried excitedly, suddenly swooping down to pick up something from the ground. It was a bit of red plastic, from a car's rear brake light. 'See, I told thee it was dragons!' he exclaimed. 'Powerful magik, dragon scales . . .' he said reverently, and was just about to put it in his pocket when he changed his mind.

Bowing deeply, he humbly offered his new treasure to Bel. 'May I give thee this, my lady?'

'Seriously!?'

'Verily! As a token of mine thanks.'

Bel took the plastic with a smile. Wilfred wasn't just excellent at keeping up his act, he was brilliantly inventive with it. *Okay, he's either a genius,* she thought. *Or . . . or he really is a wizard's apprentice from the eleventh century.*

Bel stopped walking and looked Wilfred straight in the eye. 'Wilfred, have you really come from the past?'

'Verily.'

'And you honestly were Wincewart the Withering's apprentice?'

'Verily.'

'Then how did you get here?'

'I told thee – by scrying glass.'

'So where is this scrying glass then?'

Sheer panic shot into Wilfred's face – and stayed there.

'Rabbits' rumps! I do not have it! I must have dropped it in the cave!' he cried.

Which might seem a bit clumsy, but Wilfred had never travelled by scrying glass before. And, to be fair, he wasn't even expecting to travel anywhere, anyhow or by any means, so you can't really blame him for not thinking to hang onto the crystal ball, can you?

'Yeah, right!' said Bel, rolling her eyes and thinking what an idiot she was for even beginning to think Wilfred was telling the truth.

'Nay,' persisted Wilfred, grabbing her arm, as a most dire and dreadful thought overwhelmed him. 'Thou does not understand. If I do not have a scrying glass, then how can I get back home?'

'I dunno, on the bus?' (Which was a good joke, you have to admit, but completely lost on Wilfred, who wouldn't have known what a bus was if it had run him over.)

'Would thou be able to ask Lord Jon if he could lend me one?' he asked her tentatively.

'What, a bus?' laughed Bel, deliberately misunderstanding him.

'No, my lady, a scrying glass,' Wilfred replied earnestly.

Bel shot him an odd look. 'Let me get this straight. You're telling me you actually know how to travel through time?'

'Alas no, my lady.'

'Ha!' snorted Bel triumphantly, thinking she'd finally caught him out in his act.

'But my master will know, and he will rescue me.'

'Again, seriously!?'

'Again, verily!'

The scrying glass

Jon readily let Bel borrow a scrying glass from Crystals and Cauldrons. They hurried back to the cafe, and, pausing only to help themselves to a plate of jam doughnuts, belted upstairs to her room, two at a time.

'Oi! I saw that!' laughed Gloria to their retreating backs.

Upstairs, Wilfred grabbed a doughnut, then he bowed to Bel and addressed her seriously.

'My lady, may I show thee how I can make this disappear before thy very eyes?' he said.

'Only if you can do it without setting anything on fire!' she warned.

Wilfred promptly stuffed the entire doughnut in his mouth in one go and grinned broadly.

'Idiot!' she laughed. 'But stop mucking about and get on with it. I want to see this Wincewart!' She took Jon's scrying glass out of its wooden box and looked into it wonderingly. Was she really about to see the face of a genuine, real-life wizard staring at her from a thousand years ago? A tinge of excitement shot through her.

Happily cramming another doughnut into his mouth and licking sugar off his fingers, Wilfred put out his hand for the scrying glass.

'Wilfred the Wise!' cried Bel. 'Do you want your master to see you with sugar all over your gob and jam dribbling down your chin! Look in the mirror!'

He gave her a lopsided sugary grin, and looking in the mirror, wiped his mouth on his (or rather, Wincewart's) sleeve, and licked his fingers clean.

'What do you have to do? Is there anything you need?' she asked, eager to help him.

Wilfred shrugged. 'Nay, I be only going to speak with my master and ask him to help me.'

'Through the scrying glass?'

'Verily.'

'And you can honestly do this?'

'Indeed,' said Wilfred, remembering his exchange with Wincewart in Jon's shop. Then, looking her straight in the eye, he added confidently, 'Trust me. I be a wizard!'

And for the first time, Bel honestly believed he was.

Wilfred took the scrying glass in his hand, and stepped into the chalk pentacle, which, although a bit scuffed, was still clear on the dark blue carpet.

A shiver of anticipation, almost fear, swamped Bel and her mouth went dry. Then her heart started beating quickly. She could hardly dare believe what she was about to witness.

'Shall I shut the curtains?' she whispered. But Wilfred shook his head.

Then, clutching his Bag of Bees with one hand, and with the scrying glass in the other, he stared deeply into its depths.

'Master? Art thou there?'

There was an eerie silence. Standing just outside

the pentacle, Bel looked over his shoulder and also peered intently into the crystal ball.

There was no reply. The glass was dark.

Wilfred tried again.

'Master? Can thou hear me?'

There was still no reply, so he tried again . . . and again . . . and again.

He tried commanding the crystal ball, then begging and pleading with it to get Wincewart to reply to him. But the glass remained stubbornly black.

Wilfred was gutted.

He'd always relied on Wincewart bailing him out of trouble no matter what magikal mayhem he'd caused in the past. In fact, now he stopped to think about it, he'd always relied on Wincewart for everything. If he couldn't get Wincewart to help him, then he'd be stranded here in the future – for ever. 'Buzzards' gizzards!' he cursed softly as the enormity of his problem sank in.

Bel was gutted too.

She had wanted so much to believe in Wilf's magic. She'd convinced herself that he really was an eleventh century wizard's apprentice. But he obviously wasn't. She wondered what sort of a gullible idiot she was for falling for Wilf's act, and didn't know whether to be embarrassed or irritated. *Either way, he must think I'm a right dork brain,* she cringed.

But neither had time to brood on their disappointment, because at that moment Gloria yelled up, asking them to make some chips for the lunchtime rush.

Chapter Nineteen

Ye Basic Chopping Charm

Going down to the cafe kitchen, they found a small mountain of potatoes on the side waiting to be peeled and chipped. Bel groaned, picked up the peeler and handed Wilf a knife.

'I'll peel and you chip.'

'Chip?'

'Yes, chip.'

'Not chop?

'No, chip.'

'I can chop but I know not how to chip.'

'Very funny, Wilf, but I'm not in the mood,' snapped Bel, now just annoyed that he was still pretending to be something he so obviously wasn't. 'If you can chop, you can chip. So just chop chips,' she finished crossly.

But Wilfred still appeared to be utterly baffled.

So, sighing irritably, Bel showed him how to cut the peeled spuds into chips.

It looked simple enough, but it immediately occurred to Wilf that there was an even quicker and easier way to do it. So, laying the knife on the worktop and clutching his Bag of Bees, he muttered Ye Basic Chopping Charm.

'Mighty axe, sword or blade!
And-um-this-strange-little-kitchen-knife-made-out-of-wood-and-metal-stuck-together . . .
I need thy aid!
Thou must chop till thou stop,
And then thou may drop.'

There was a quick flash of lightning and a flicker of coloured sparks, and, to Bel's stunned surprise, the knife jumped up from the worktop and promptly proceeded to chop the potatoes into chips.

All by itself.

O-M-G!

Bel froze. Her eyes widened. She forgot to breathe. 'How? How are you doing that?' she whispered, as the kitchen knife efficiently sliced its way through a large potato and moved onto the next one.

Wilf shrugged modestly. 'With Ye Basic Chopping Charm. I use it every day on the axe to chop the kindling.'

Bel turned slowly to look at him. She took in his scruffy hair, his grubby face, his tunic and leggings, and his tatty old boots and his rather spectacular blue and gold cloak.

'O-M-G. You really are a wizard,' she gasped, awestruck.

'A mere apprentice,' he reminded her humbly.

'From the past,' she stammered.

'Verily, a thousand years ago.'

'And you actually, literally and genuinely lived with Wincewart the Withering . . .'

'The most powerful wizard in all Wallop in the Wold,' nodded Wilfred.

'Again, O-M-G,' finished Bel.

He grinned at her delightedly.

Chopping and chipping

Meanwhile, the knife had finished chipping the potatoes Bel had peeled and had moved onto another one.

'No, wait! I have to peel them first!' she laughed.

But the knife carried on chopping cheerfully.

'Wait! Hang on!' said Bel.

But it didn't, and soon it had cut so many chips they started to tumble off the worktop and onto the floor.

'Wilf, make it stop!' cried Bel.

The grin on Wilfred's face froze as he realised that he didn't know how to stop Ye Basic Chopping Charm. Back in the hermit cave the axe just stopped chopping automatically when it ran out of firewood. But there were sackfuls of spuds in the cafe.

More and more chips toppled to the floor and tumbled across the floor.

'Wilf! Do something!' begged Bel urgently.

'I cannot! I know not what to do!'

'For crying out loud, Wilf!'

Panic-stricken, Wilfred ran his fingers through his hair and tried to think.

'Can't you just reverse the spell?' cried Bel, as the heap of chips began to engulf the kitchen floor.

'My lady! That is *precisely* what my master would do! But alas I know not how! Do thou know?

'No! I don't! Try doing it backwards or something!' she begged.

Which was easier said than done, or rather, easier done than said. It was easy to do the actions in reverse order, but saying the words backwards was the tricky bit. And let's be honest, Wilfred usually struggled to say them the right way anyway.

Wilfred desperately tried to repeat Ye Basic Chopping Charm backwards. After a few goes he managed it, and to their enormous relief, the knife stopped mid-chop and clattered down harmlessly onto the kitchen surface.

Then, the improbable quantity of chips faded and vanished until there was just the modest pile Wilfred had cut.

'No harm done.' said Wilfred cheerfully. 'Yet thou must think me a dolt and a lummox for messing up such basik magik!'

'No comment,' said Bel, and, pointedly handing him the knife, added, 'Let's start again. And as I said, I'll peel and you chip.'

Sheepishly, Wilfred did as he was told.

When they'd finished, Bel called through to Gloria in the cafe. 'Mum! We've done the chips! See you later!' And then she yanked Wilfred out of the kitchen and dragged him off before he caused any more chaos.

A grimoire?

They headed to the castle. Wilf sat on a low, grassy mound of rubble, which was all that remained of the great outer wall, and gloomily worried about the future, in more ways than one.

'Wilf, are you listening to me?' said Bel.

It was a question Wincewart had often asked Wilfred. (And in case you're interested, he usually wasn't.)

Bel plonked herself down next to him. 'Listen – you don't *need* Wincewart's help to get back to your own time,' she explained excitedly. 'If you can undo a spell by reversing it – like you did with the chips – then all you have to do is do whatever you did you get here, but do it *backwards*!'

Wilf's grubby face lit up and a huge grin slowly spread across it.

'My lady,' he cried, 'thou art most clever! Why did I not think of that? Truly I be an idiot!'

'Again, no comment,' joked Bel. 'Right, then,' she added in a business-like tone. 'What *exactly* did you do to get here?'

Wilfred thought hard. It was entertaining to watch him. He frowned, looked up at his scruffy fringe for inspiration, and did a lot of lip chewing. But after a while his face fell. 'Alas, I cannot remember!'

'Seriously?' cried Bel, who, had she known him better, would have known that his inability to remember *any* spell with accuracy was always going to be the flaw in her otherwise excellent plan.

By the time Bel had mastered a piece of magic, she'd practised it so often she knew it completely by heart. But the way Wilfred studied magik was, well . . . it was all a bit more hit and miss. (With far more misses that hits.)

'So you didn't actually learn the spell?' cried Bel.

'No! There was no need!' cried Wilfred indignantly. 'I took it from Wincewart's grimoire!'

'His *what*?'

'His big, red leather-bound *Ye Ancient Yet Complete Runic Record of Magik Charms and Enchantments.*

'Again, his *what*?'

'His spell book.'

'Okay, fine – so where's the book?'

Wilf winced. 'I do not have it, my lady . . .'

Gobsmackingly stupid

'Let me get this straight, you travelled a thousand years into the future –'

'By scrying glass,' interrupted Wilf.

'By scrying glass,' repeated Bel flatly, 'and using a book. But you didn't think to bring either the scrying glass or the book with you?'

Wilfred cringed. When she put it like that, it did seem fairly foolish. (Bel would have gone with 'gobsmackingly stupid'!)

'How did you think you were going to get back?'

'But I did not know I was going to *come* to the future,' exclaimed Wilfred. 'I only asked the scrying glass to *show* me the future. Methinks I must have done something wrong!'

'You think? Oh, good grief.' Bel rolled her eyes.

'Dungbeetles' bottoms! cried Wilfred, grabbing her arm eagerly. A sudden and brilliant idea had struck him. 'The grimoire! It will be hidden in Wincewart's cave! My master always cast Ye Cheap

Yet Cheerful Concealing Charm upon it to keep it safe from other wizards.

'Don't be daft, Wilf – that was a thousand years ago. It will have been eaten by rats and mice ages ago, or probably just crumbled into dust.'

'Aha! But my lady, it will not! A spell book is enchanted. It can never be destroyed!' Wilfred's eyes shone with excitement and a huge grin lit his grubby face.

'Is that a fact?' said Bel sceptically.

'Verily so.'

'But the cave is just a legend!'

'It be not "just a legend"!' snapped Wilfred hotly. 'It be my home.' And, slinging Bel's rucksack over his shoulder, he scrambled to his feet and raced off.

'Hey – where are you going?'

'Home!' Wilfred called back cheerfully. Bel leapt up and followed, holding onto her hat as she ran.

The long-lost cave of Wincewart the Withering

Wilfred headed for the point where the hillside suddenly dropped away. A steep, stone path zigzagged down the grassy slope, and he hurtled down it so quickly he nearly fell into the dense bramble thicket at the bottom. He looked about to get his bearings. Then, snatching up a broken branch, Wilf launched a violent and unprovoked attack on the defenceless blackberries.

By the time Bel caught him up, he'd smashed his way through the bush almost to the rocky hillside behind. Suddenly she heard him give a whoop of triumph. 'Parsnips' pustules!'

'What? WHAT?' she called.

'It be here!'

Bel eyed the mangled tangle of bushes. 'Oh, for crying out loud! The way to the cave is through the biggest blackberry bush in all of Withering Wallop in the Wold?'

'Verily!' called Wilfred.

'Oh brilliant,' she muttered, gingerly pushing aside the sharp brambles to follow him. (If I'm honest, she was less worried by the thought of the vicious blackberry thorns scratching her to pieces, than she was by the thought of enormous hairy spiders dropping down her neck.)

When she'd finally managed to scrabble through, she found Wilfred standing in the entrance to a cave, waiting for her. Proudly, he took her hand and led her inside.

'Dungbeetles' droppings!' she gasped.

The entrance opened out into a large cave. It was a bit gloomy, but there was some light spilling in from cracks high up in the rocks.

'Welcome to mine humble home, my lady,' bowed Wilfred with a grin.

Bumblebees' buttocks!

Okay, so as homes went, it was extremely modest by modern standards. (But then, it was extremely modest by mediaeval standards too.) It was just the one room, with no electricity or running water . . . or windows. . . or furniture . . . and, crucially, no loo.

But Bel could clearly see it had once been lived in. There was a fireplace, still sooted and full of ash. And what looked like stumps of candle stumps lay dusty and abandoned on the dirty floor, together with shards of broken bits of pots and bottles.

'This really is it, isn't it?' she muttered incredulously, turning to Wilfred, astounded. 'It's Wincewart the Withering's cave!'

You'd have thought Wilfred would have been elated, but as a matter of fact, he was gutted. The true enormity of having travelled a millennium ahead of his time hit him like . . . well, like a well-aimed fresh cowpat.

Yes, he'd found the hermit cave. But there was nothing, and no one, there. No Wincewart the Withering, no Bertram the Beady, no cauldrons, no table or chair, no chests or boxes of enchantment ingredients, or bits of wizarding kit and caboodle – not even a shrivelled mangel-wurzel or a dried-up hunk of bread.

And there was absolutely and definitely *no* grimoire.

And, strangely, foolishly, even, he really hadn't expected that.

'Bumblebees' buttocks!' he cried in disappointment. He also said a couple of other, much ruder words, which, fortunately, Bel didn't know.

(But, just in case you do know them, I'm not going to put what he said.)

A modest home

Determined to look on the bright side, Wilfred thought that at least he had found his home, so he announced cheerfully, 'I shall live here, my lady.'

'You can't!' exclaimed Bel.

'I be not going back to the campsite!' he insisted.

'But it's . . . its . . . a cave!'

'It be not much,' agreed Wilfred humbly, looking around. 'But it be mine home! And to me, it be . . . "awesome"!'

'Hmmm. Not exactly "Home, Sweet Home", though, is it?' said Bel. So she decided to take Wilfred back to the Enchanted Cave Cafe to pick up some supplies.

She made a mental list as they went: sleeping bag, pillow, broom, dustpan and brush, bin liner, wind-up torch, sausages, bread, ketchup, juice, biscuits, candles (she wouldn't bother with matches) and . . . er . . . loo paper? she wondered, but understandably, didn't like to ask Wilfred if he actually wanted any – or even knew what it was – or how to use it.

(And she certainly wasn't going to tell him if he didn't.)

Chapter Twenty

Wincewart the Listless

Gloomily, Wincewart crumbled the remains of the dried loaf onto his wooden platter. He hadn't touched the nettle soup Bertram had made for his lunch. Partly because it was barely edible, but mostly because he wasn't in the mood to eat.

His familiar flapped down and perched on the arm of the great chair. He regarded his master anxiously. The merrymaking was tomorrow and Wincewart was meant to be providing the hundreds of merrymakers with a breathtakingly spectacular finale – but here he was, moping around, and looking about as spectacular as a wet sack.

It did not bode well.

After a while the canny raven spoke, choosing his words carefully. 'What will thou do at the merrymaking if thou cannot do Ye Spectacular Disappearing Enchantment?' he cawed.

Wincewart shrugged listlessly.

'More to the point,' added the raven, cocking his head to one side, 'What will Lord Wallop do to thee?'

Wincewart shuddered visibly and then positively flinched when he imagined what the Lady Wallop would do to him. He suspected that whatever it was, it would definitely be painful and probably involve the legendary rod of iron. 'I do not dare to think,' he winced.

'The Lord Wallop will surely replace thee,' croaked Bertram glumly. 'I hear Rufus the Rueful and his rude apprentice Rory the Rollicking art looking for work. And I know the Lady Wallop was mightily impressed by Grumblegroin the Great and his gifted novice Griffin the Grave when last they visited the castle.'

Putting his white-haired head in his hands, Wincewart groaned pathetically.

'Master, thou must pull thyself together!' squawked Bertram urgently. 'Thou do not have time to mope around. Thou must do something!'

'What do thou suggest?' asked Wincewart hopelessly.

The raven ruffled his feathers importantly and fixed his beady eye on the elderly wizard. 'Thou will just have to master Ye Astonishing Disappearing Enchantment *without* thy dragon's claw talisman,' he cawed.

'Easier said than done,' harrumphed Wincewart.

'But, master, thou does not need trinkets and talismans to aid thee!' coaxed the raven. 'Thou art Wincewart the Withering, Castle Mage, Soothsaying Sage and the greatest wizard in all Wallop in the Wold! Surely thou art not going to allow the loss of a mere silver bauble to defeat thee?'

'Creaking cauldrons! Thou art right!' announced Wincewart, rising to his feet. 'I be a mighty wizard! Grabbing his grimoire, and the necessary magikal kit and caboodle, Wincewart strode outside to practise Ye Astonishing Disappearing Enchantment – *without* his talisman of potency.

Bertram sighed with relief.

A thick fog on the hillside

Some time later, and, if I'm honest, after a little nap, Bertram fluttered outside to see how the mighty mage was getting on.

It all *looked* impressive enough, as Wincewart stood with his dark cloak billowing majestically around him, waving his staff and chanting commandingly away amidst torrents of multicoloured sparks, bolts of lightning, and a thick fog of bright purple smoke. But was it working?

The snag with practising a vanishing spell on yourself, on your own and long before mirrors have been invented, is that it's difficult to know how you're getting on.

Looking at his nose with both eyes at once, Wincewart was convinced he couldn't see it at all. So that was promising. Worryingly though, Wincewart could still see the rest of his body . . . but could anyone else?

'Bertram!' he called as the raven fluttered to the ground in front of him. 'Can thou see me?'

'Yes,' replied the raven, strutting along the grass.

'Art thou sure?'

'Thou has not disappeared even one tiny bit!' cawed Bertram. 'But thy beard looks a lot shorter than it used to be!' he added cheekily.

Wincewart harrumphed.

Bertram cocked his head cannily. 'Master, I have an idea!'

Wincewart stopped chanting and turned to his familiar. 'Thou do?'

'Verily. Methinks thou should use trickery at the merrymaking.'

'Trickery?'

'Other wizards do. Thou could create a screen of smoke and colourful sparks and then, perchance using a secret trap door, or a curtain, thou could at least *seem* to disappear.'

'Trickery! TRICKERY? Tangled talismans! I be a wizard, not a . . . trickster!' spluttered Wincewart, deeply offended.

Eleventh century Wallop in the Wold was littered with unscrupulous tricksters: cheats, swindlers, charlatans and frauds, most of whom claimed to be 'wizards' of some sort or another. But most of whom were in the thieving trade. They were bringing the sorcery business a bad name.

'Have it thy own way!' retorted Bertram. 'I was only trying to aid thee.' And he fluttered off to his perch to sulk.

Chapter Twenty-One

Wilfred the Joyful

A choking, dry cloud of ancient ash billowed up from the long-abandoned fireplace in the hermit cave as Wilfred busily cleaned it out.

'These be mighty clever tools,' he said eagerly. 'What did thou call them?'

'A dustpan and brush,' replied Bel straight-faced, as she set up the camp bed on the stone floor.

'A "dustpan",' repeated Wilfred reverently. 'I have not seen one before.'

Bel had begun to realise there were a great many

things Wilfred hadn't seen before. Like a hairbrush, a bar of soap and a flannel for a start. She was idly wondering what he'd make of having a bath or a shower when suddenly he yelled out.

'Wizards' pimples! JOY BE MINE!' And he started dancing round the cave like a lunatic. 'I have found it!'

'What?'

Wilfred thrust his grubby hand towards her. Lying in his palm, covered in ash, was a sort-of brooch.

She peered closely. 'What is it?'

'Ah, thou cannot see it clearly!' He took a quick deep breath and blew the ash off it – straight up Bel's nose.

'Maggots' mumps, Wilf!' she choked, waving the ash dust away.

'My lady, I do be sorry!' he cried, but his eyes were shining with excitement. 'It be my master's dragon's claw talisman!'

(In case you're wondering how the eleventh century talisman ended up in the fireplace in the hermit cave in the twenty-first century, I'll try to explain: it didn't. It actually landed in the fireplace in the *eleventh* century when Wilfred's attempt at Ye Spectacular Summoning Spell went spectacularly

wrong, right at the very beginning. (By which I mean the beginning of the story – not the beginning of the eleventh century. Are you with me so far? It's complicated, I know, but try to keep up.)

Of course it was way too hot for anyone to search for the talisman in the flames – even if they'd thought to look there, which they didn't. So the talisman was *still* in the fireplace, lost in the ash for centuries, until Wilfred finally got round to clearing out the fire a thousand years later. See? And yes, I do realise a thousand years is a long time not to clean out a fireplace.)

'I lost the talisman yesterday,' Wilfred explained to Bel, 'and my master did threaten me with a dire and dreadful fate if I did not find it!'

'Sounds like a nice man,' observed Bel dryly. 'I can see why you're so keen to go back to him.'

'Ah, but thou do not understand. This be his greatest treasure. He wears it all the time.'

'Hang on a minute,' said Bel. 'If you lost it yesterday, then how come you just found it in the fireplace? We only came in here an hour ago?'

Wilfred immediately saw the reason for her confusion and, nodding wisely (or rather, nodding in a way that he hoped made him *look* wise) he tried to explain.

'I did not lose the talisman in *thy* yesterday. I lost it *my* yesterday. Does thou see?'

'No, I don't. Possibly because you're not making any sense!'

'*Thy* yesterday was yesterday ago, but *my* yesterday was a thousand years ago,' he explained, or rather, tried to explain. (Technically of course it was a thousand years and a day ago, but what's a day between millennia?)

'But "thy" yesterday *is* "my" yesterday, or rather it *was*, and anyway whose ever it was, it was still only yesterday!' cried Bel with mounting irritation.

It was Wilf's turn to be confused. (Strictly speaking it wasn't his turn – he'd had far more goes at being confused than Bel had over the last day or so, but who's counting?)

'Wilf, have you had a bump on the head lately?' Bel finished sarcastically.

'I do not think so . . .' He shrugged, then grinned

and picked up the rucksack. Then he carefully took out the scrying glass. 'Crows' kneecaps! My master's joy will know no bounds when I tell him I have found his talisman.' With trembling, grimy hands, he cradled the scrying glass and peered into it. But again, the glass was dark. 'Master?' he called tentatively. 'Master, art thou there?'

Bel peered over his shoulder, but there was nothing to see.

'Looks like he art not,' she said dryly.

The crystal ball contained nothing except their reflections on blackness. Which wasn't surprising, because of course back in the eleventh century, Wincewart's scrying glass was shut inside the darkness of its wooden box. Ironically, it was about only two feet away from them. (Well, about two feet and one thousand years away.) So near and yet so far!

Disappointed, Wilfred set the crystal ball on a stone ledge and gave up.

'Come on,' said Bel suddenly. 'Let's get a fire going for the sausages. 'Put that talisman thing somewhere safe so you don't lose it again.'

Wilfred certainly didn't want to lose it again. Losing it twice in two days would be ridiculously unlucky – careless, even. (Although technically he would only be losing it twice in a thousand years. Which doesn't sound quite so bad, does it?)

Chewing his lip, he considered the safest place to stash the dragon's claw. Not the pocket of Wincewart's cloak – it could slip out far too easily. How about inside one of his boots? But what if he trod on it and broke it? The only secure place he could think of was *inside* his Bag of Bees magik charm. With trembling fingers, he cautiously pulled open the top of the pouch. He'd have to be quick so as not to risk any of the bees escaping. But thankfully, the bees didn't seem to be awake (or possibly even alive), so he hurriedly slipped the talisman inside and tied the bag back up. Then he went out to fetch kindling.

A blazing fire

Having piled a good stack of wood into the fireplace, Wilf clutched his Bag of Bees and chanted Ye Simple Lighting Spell. There was a terrifyingly loud crack of thunder, and a brilliant flash of lightning, and instantly a roaring blaze erupted, filling the fireplace with two-foot-high flames. An immense amount of turquoise smoke also billowed into the cave.

'Wooaah!' cried Bel, leaping back from the blaze with the pan of sausages.

Wilfred was stunned. Although he was definitely beginning to get the hang of Ye Simple Lighting Spell, he'd never managed to create such an impressive roaring fire before. (Which might have been because he'd been practising – but then again, it might not.)

'You've *so* got to teach me how to do that!' demanded Bel.

He promised he would, but after supper. Then he insisted on cooking the sausages on the fire *himself*. (Not because he was being polite, or because he liked cooking, but because he'd already set one wizard on fire and didn't want to risk doing it again.)

A short while later, munching on crunchy, charred sausages, Bel invited Wilfred to go to the Midsummer Madness Wizarding and Witchcraft Festival with her and Jon the next day.

'Awesome!' cried Wilfred excitedly. Finally, after a thousand years, he was going to the merrymaking!

'It'll mean getting up very early, to set up the stall,' she warned him.

Wilfred shrugged – he was used to rising at dawn. 'Will thou be performing thy magic?' he asked, wiping sausage fat off his chin with his sleeve (technically, Wincewart's sleeve.)

'No, we'll just be selling stuff from the shop.'

'But thou should! Thou art a highly skilled wizard!'

'Trust me, I'm not a wizard!' laughed Bel. 'And anyway, I'm not good enough yet. But you are.'

'I be not!' spluttered Wilfred, with a really good attempt at false modesty.

'Yes you "be"!'

'Not!'

'Be!'

'Be I really?' he cried excitedly. 'Do thou think I am – truly?'

'Yeah! Honest. I mean, badgers' butts, Wilf! That fire lighting thing you do is awesome. And, hey – you promised to show me how to do it!'

A blazing row

Wilfred spent the next hour or so patiently trying to teach Bel how to do Ye Simple Lighting Spell. Well, strictly speaking that's not true. After about ten minutes his patience had worn thin and by the end of the hour he was exasperated beyond measure.

Bel tried. She really, really tried and, in fact, she wanted to go on trying until she could do it. But the candle stubbornly refused to light, and it probably won't surprise you to learn that it was Wilfred who gave up first.

'I cannot understand why thou cannot do it!' he snapped irritably. ''Tis but basik magik – as old as the hills.'

'Maybe that's the problem,' sighed Bel.

'I cannot teach you anything more difficult if thou cannot master basik magik!' retorted Wilfred, misunderstanding her and unintentionally sounding a lot like Wincewart.

'No, I didn't mean that. I meant maybe I can't do it because it's magic. *Real* magic. You know, genuine-eleventh-century-magic-that-only-genuine-eleventh-century-wizards-can-do?'

'I do not understand thee,' said Wilfred, his grubby face even more clouded with confusion than usual.

'Well, I can't do *real* magic, can I?'

He looked at her, totally bewildered.

'My magic's just tricks, isn't it?' Bel spelled out painfully.

It took a few seconds for the meaning of what Bel had said to sink in.

'Tricks?' he gasped reeling backwards. 'Thy magik is trickery?'

'Well, of course it is!'

Wilfred was thunderstruck. 'But . . . but that be deceit and deception, fakery and falseness and . . . cheating! Thou art not a wizard! Thou art *a trickster and fraud*!' he spluttered hotly.

'Oh, don't hold back, will you?' snapped Bel.

'Thou lied to me!'

'No, I didn't!'

'Thou pretended to be a wizard.'

'I did not!' she retorted hotly. 'I kept saying I wasn't! What was it about the phrase "Trust me, I'm not a wizard!" that made you think I was a wizard, for crying out loud!' Bel got to her feet angrily.

'My lady, I did not mean to offend thee,' cried Wilfred, getting up too.

'Seriously?' fumed Bel. 'SERIOUSLY? So just what is it about the phrase "thou art a trickster and fraud" that wasn't meant to offend me?' She turned on her heels and stormed off.

'Can I still come to the merrymaking with thee?' he called after her hopefully. (You have to admire his optimism. Seriously.)

'NO!' she hurled furiously over her shoulder as she left.

Wilfred was gutted. Not only was he going to missing the merrymaking for the second time in a thousand years, but he'd upset the best friend he'd ever had. Also in a thousand years.

'Dragons' farts!' he groaned, and sank back down to sit cross-legged on the ground with his head in his hands. 'Wilfred the Wise, thou be an idiot.'

For a while he sat brooding by the fire, in the darkening cave, gloomily watching the moon rise outside.

Chapter Twenty-Two

Wincewart in despair

As night fell, the moon rose above the hermit cave. (Just to make it clear, it was the same moon, and the same cave, but a different millennium.) Wincewart stood at the entrance, staring out at the dark hillside and hoping (actually, make that 'desperately longing') to see Wilfred come sloping homeward. And, more importantly, bringing the missing talisman with him.

But as the darkness deepened, he saw only the ruins of his reputation and fortunes staring back at him.

The elderly wizard went miserably back into the

cave, and sank into his chair in despair. 'Ominous omens and jangled jinxes! I be doomed! Doomed!' he cried. 'What can I do? Lord Wallop has told all, from the lowliest peasant to the most noble lord, that I will vanish before their very eyes in the most spectacular finale to the Midsummer Merrymaking of Magik and Mages there has ever been. What will happen when I do not?'

Bertram was tactless enough to tell him. 'The lowly peasants will pelt thee with soggy tomatoes, mouldy lettuces and rotten cabbages. The noble lords will point their fingers and laugh at thee fit to burst their tunics, and Lord Wallop will be so furious that he will throw thee out, order thee never to darken the doors of his castle again, and banish thee altogether from Wallop in the Wold. By this hour on the morrow thou will be homeless and penniless and ruined. And so will I. Trust me, I be a raven!' he croaked miserably.

Wincewart groaned and closed his eyes. He simply couldn't bear to think about what the future might bring.

'But if thou look on the bright side,' squawked Bertram, 'Lady Wallop might just solve all thy problems.'

'How?' asked Wincewart eagerly, opening his eyes and sitting forward.

'By slaughtering you on the spot.'

The raven wasn't exaggerating. It was rumoured the tiny woman could fell a full-size knight with a sharp look and a shrill shriek.

Wincewart groaned again.

Bertram hopped along the table to where the scrying glass lay in its box and rapped on it sharply with his beak.

'Methinks thou need to speak to Wilfred *nicely* and ask him to come back – and to bring thy talisman with him.'

'What if he says no?'

The canny raven cocked his head to one side and fixed his master with a steely eye. 'Then thou will have to beg.'

Wincewart winced.

'Thou might even have to apologise.'

Wincewart literally flinched. His left eye was twitching uncontrollably, but he could recognise the wisdom of his familiar's words, even though it would be painful – no, make that *excruciating agony* – to have to apologise to his apprentice.

'But did thou not see the riches his new master

has?' Wincewart sulked. 'How can I compete with that?'

'Thou will have to bribe him to lure him back,' replied Bertram. 'Offer him a pay rise. How much does thou pay him?'

'Half a mangel-wurzel a week.'

Bertram wasn't convinced that even offering a *whole* mangel-wurzel a week would be a big enough incentive to entice Wilfred back. He thought for a moment, then suggested, 'How about thou gives him a whole wurzel every week, a woollen blanket, *and* his own piece of chalk? And let him whistle on Saturdays? But quietly.'

The ancient wizard sighed. 'Fine. But I shall give him *nothing* if he does not have my dragon's claw talisman,' he warned. 'And he must not whistle until I have woken up!'

Bertram nodded. It seemed like a fair deal.

Wincewart swallowed his pride. (Which, frankly, was a remarkable feat.) Taking his scrying glass out of its box, he stared into its mysterious depths and chanted Ye Very Ancient Seeing Spell.

Swirls of deep-blue smoke flooded the crystal ball, and then cleared to reveal . . .

Wilfred, sitting cross-legged on the floor in a cave,

in front of a blazing fire, staring mournfully at the moon.

'WILFRED!' yelled Wincewart.

Wincewart be doomed

At the sound of the wizard's voice, thin and weedy though it sounded, Wilfred leapt joyously to his feet. 'Master!' he cried, looking around the cave in confusion. 'Where art thou?'

'Dolthead! I be here – in the scrying glass!'

Wilfred eagerly swept up the crystal ball.

And a thousand years away, Wincewart the Withering, the most powerful wizard in all of eleventh century Wallop in the Wold, took a deep breath. Then, shuddering with indignity, he prepared to apologise to his dolthead of an apprentice.

But he couldn't.

Because Wilfred was so busily rummaging around in his Bag of Bees charm, and speaking so excitedly at him, that he couldn't get a word in edgeways. Truth be told, he could barely follow the gabbling gibberish.

But then one thing suddenly became very clear to him. His silver dragon's claw talisman – which

Wilfred was holding in his grubby hand towards the crystal ball!

'JOY BE MINE!' thundered the wizard in a voice loud enough to travel across an entire millennium. 'Thou has found it! I be not doomed! Wilfred, if thou come back to the hermit cave right now, and bring it with thee, I will forgive thee everything.' (He made no mention of a pay rise, a woollen blanket, his own piece of chalk, or the chance to whistle quietly on Saturdays, you will notice.)

'But, master,' stammered Wilfred nervously, 'I cannot! I know not how!'

'Why not? Where art thou?'

'I be in thy cave master, but *in the future*! I told thee!' And, holding the crystal ball in his open palm, Wilfred slowly twirled around to reveal his surroundings to Wincewart.

It would be fair to say that the wizard had never been more astonished in his life. It had never occurred to him that Wilfred had the talent to enchant his way out of a wet sack, never mind all the way into the future. *By the ulcers of Ulric the Ultimate! He was telling the truth,* Wincewart thought, truly amazed.

'How . . . how did thou get there?' he stammered in awe.

'With a foretelling spell, but I cannot remember which one.' Wilfred sheepishly hung his head. 'It was from thy spell book. Can thou rescue me? I want to come home,' he begged.

Wincewart doubted very much he could do such high magik – especially without his talisman. But he didn't want to admit that to his apprentice.

'Er . . . thou will have to wait until I have consulted the grimoire, and studied the necessary enchantment, and, er . . . gathered the charm ingredients. And it will depend on the moon and the stars and, er . . . the weather. Methinks I may be some time. Do not wait up,' he blustered.

The scrying glass went dark.

Happy in the knowledge that his master would surely rescue him soon, Wilfred pulled Bel's camp bed over to the fire, lay down on it and went to sleep.

Wincewart, on the other hand, went berserk.

'Idiot, stupid, lumpen, foolish, dunderheaded fool of an apprentice!' he roared. 'How many times have I told him not to meddle with magik he does not understand! And now he has actually and astonishingly stranded himself in the future *with* my dragon's claw talisman, and I cannot get either of them back *without* it.'

Wincewart paced furiously up and down the hermit cave, shaking his fists and raging wrathfully for several minutes non-stop. Then he swore by the hexes of Hagbane the Horrible, and by the blisters of Bladderwart the Blunt, and by the enchanted spindle of Rumplecrispskin the Ridiculous that he would turn his aforementioned idiot, stupid, lumpen, foolish, dunderheaded fool of an apprentice into a giant common-or-garden slug with the face of a sheep, the brain of a minnow and the bray of a donkey. Well, that is, if he ever got his hands on him again.

Bertram confined his thoughts to a single, brief sentence. 'Thou art doomed!'

Suddenly deflated, Wincewart sank wearily into his chair. Bertram was right. He, Wincewart the Withering, Castle Mage, Soothsaying Sage and the greatest wizard in all Wallop in the Wold, was doomed.

Chapter Twenty-Three

A healthy breakfast

At dawn the next morning, a yawning Bel was helping her dad load up the van outside Crystals and Cauldrons.

'Hey, I thought your new mate was going to pitch up to help?' said Jon. He was staggering under a stack of plastic boxes filled with charms, amulets, mugs, candlesticks and other such magical sundries, all packed between layers of T-shirts to keep them from breaking.

'Nope,' said Bel, following him with a large zip-up

bag full of talismans, charm scrolls and spell candles.

'So, like, er . . . did you fall out?'

'Yup.'

'O-kay. Er . . . awkward moment. Guess we'll have to go with the flow on that one. Shame, I thought his awesome banter and funky outfit would draw in the punters. Guess we'll just have to rely on my awesome banter and your funky outfit, kiddo!'

'In that case, we're doomed!' announced Bel, managing to give her dad a grin. 'Is that everything?'

'Yup!' Jon locked the shop door.

Bel slung her rucksack into the foot-well of the van, then clambered in.

'Okay, dudette. Wagons roll!' Jon crunched the van into gear and pulled away. 'First stop, the Enchanted Cave Cafe for a nourishing, healthy breakfast. Bacon, sausages and beans, two eggs – sunny side up – and a couple of slices of fried bread. No, make that three slices, all washed down with a good slug of gut-rotting caffeine.'

'And a bucket of hot chocolate with squirty cream and marshmallows, and a bag of jam doughnuts for me,' said Bel.

'Awesome! Like I said, a healthy breakfast.'

*

Bel gets B-Dazzled

Half an hour or so later, Jon's van was crawling up the track to the castle behind dozens of other vehicles, all heading to the festival.

The castle was already a scene of frenzied activity, as hundreds of people milled around or wrestled with rickety fold-up tables and chairs and pop-up gazebos. Empty cardboard boxes, polythene bags and zip-up holdalls lay strewn everywhere. It looked like a badly organised giant car boot sale – and a very scruffy one at that.

A row had broken out between two rival burger vans for the best pitch near the stage, while various event organisers were intent on staging the sound system battle of the millennium to see who could drown everyone else out. Barbecues were cooking up breakfast burgers at full pelt, and a huge hog roast had been cooking since the early hours. The cool morning air was laced with the smell of hot chocolate, hot dogs, and hot engine oil.

It was mayhem.

Bel and Jon dumped the van in the car park and lugged everything to their pitch in the main marquee. The tent was massive, and it took them a while to find their stall, but eventually they saw, pinned to a table, a sheet of paper labelled *Crystals and Cauldrons*.

They were crammed in between the tables for Here Be Dragons and Masquerade Magik. Opposite them stood the stalls Enchanted Cupcakes and Global Magic Inc., and next to that was a naff pop-up fortune-teller's tent, with a hand-painted sign on it that read *Mystik Kristal – the Ball sees All*.

The opening of the tent was tied back to reveal Mystik Kristal herself, in full stage make-up, a headscarf and huge hoop earrings. She sat hunched over a large, tacky glow-in-the-dark crystal ball placed on a black tablecloth, and she was slurping coffee out of a polystyrene cup.

Jon and Bel exchanged looks and tried not to laugh.

'Awesome dragons, man!' said Jon to the bloke running Here Be Dragons. His stall displayed about a dozen pottery dragons, covered with tiny metallic scales and gemstone eyes.

'Thanks!' smiled the man. 'They're handmade.'

Bel picked one up, turned it over to see the price label, then put it down again *extremely carefully*

– on the grounds that it was *extremely expensive*.

'More like "awesome prices",' she muttered to Jon privately, rolling her eyes.

Jon covered their table with a midnight-blue cloth covered in gold magic symbols, then he and Bel laid out their goods and shoved the half-emptied boxes underneath. When they'd finished, Bel drifted over to check out Masquerade Magik.

'Do me a favour – hold onto that, will you?' said the woman running the stall.

'Sure!' said Bel. She held a display board steady while the woman covered it with photos of kids with painted faces. The designs were all based on a magical theme – cats, witches and dragons, moons, stars and rainbows, and she used lot of dark colours with gold and silver highlighting.

'Snazzy,' said Bel.

'I'll do you a quick one if you like – for free for helping.'

'Yeah, cool!' nodded Bel eagerly.

'How about that one?'

'Awesome!' said Bel, then she sat on the edge of the table while the woman skilfully painted an elaborate pattern of swirls and stars in black, white and gold over Bel's left eyebrow and down the side of her face. Then the woman dug out a mirror and set it up on the table.

'Like it?'

'Wow! It's . . . it's . . . B-Dazzling!' announced Bel with a huge grin.

'Tell you what, you can sit there all day – you're a great advert for me!' joked the woman.

'Hey, don't poach the staff! I need her to drum up some punters over here!' laughed Jon from across the aisle.

Bel grinned and went back to join her dad.

Another healthy breakfast

Long after sunrise, Wilfred woke up in the cave, a bit surprised to find himself still in the twenty-first century. It began to dawn on him that Wincewart might not be able to get him back as easily, or as soon, as he wanted. Which, given the fact that he had no food, would ideally have been in time for breakfast.

Wilf's belly was grumbling louder than a pack of motorbikes on full throttle. He suddenly remembered the coin Bel had given him. So, whistling cheerfully once more, he crammed his belongings into the rucksack, slung it over his shoulder and set off into Withering Wallop in the Wold.

Gloria was surprised to see him at the Enchanted Cave Cafe. 'I thought you were up at the festival with Bel?' she said, busily serving customers.

'Ah. There was a small change of plan,' replied Wilfred, embarrassed to admit that he and Bel had fallen out. So, hurriedly choosing a very large sausage roll, two Danish pastries, a chocolate bar and packet of crisps, he handed Gloria his precious pound coin.

'Be that enough?' he asked anxiously.

Not really! thought Gloria. 'Yes, it's fine!' she lied, plonking a carton of orange juice on top of everything and adding, 'Are you going up to the festival now?'

It might seem ridiculous, but it hadn't even occurred to Wilfred that he could actually go on his own. But now he came to think of it – why shouldn't he? A huge grin lit up his grubby face. 'Yay!' he yelled, improbably excited. 'I be going to the merrymaking!' And he went off whistling cheerfully, but horribly out of tune.

Gloria watched him leave and smiled. 'Yeah, like I said, a bit weird – but nice!'

Wilfred headed towards the castle, but as he passed the library a profoundly important thought hit him like a bolt of lightning. 'Buzzards' gizzards!' he cried out loud. 'I be a dolt and a dunderhead! Surely that be where Wincewart's spell book will be!' And he pushed open the heavy oak door and went inside.

The long-suffering librarian of Withering Wallop in the Wold was used to the annual invasion of witches and wizards during festival week – especially their raging hordes of bored and fractious offspring. So she wasn't too surprised when a boy wearing a wizard's cloak several sizes too big for him appeared at her desk and said he was looking for a book of magic spells.

'Did you want any one in particular?' she queried, peering over the top of her glasses.

'Wincewart the Withering's grimoire.'

'Wincewart . . . the . . . Withering's . . . Grimoire . . .' repeated the librarian as she typed it into the computer search system. Then she shook her head. 'Sorry, I can't find any book called *Wincewart the Withering's Grimoire*.'

'It be not *called* 'Wincewart's Grimoire'!' laughed Wilfred, 'It *be* Wincewart's grimoire!'

'O-kay . . . Um, do you happen to know what it *is* called?'

'Nay, I be sorry, but I do not,' he said, giving her his trademark lopsided and sheepish grin.

'Well, in that case I'm sorry, but I probably can't help you.'

'But thou must have all the books in the world here!' declared Wilfred.

'Er . . . no. We're quite a small library really!' she smiled.

'Thou art being modest! No matter, I shall have to look myself.'

'Well, the books about magic are over there,' she said, pointing helpfully. 'Hope you find it!' she added kindly.

'Oh, I will! Trust me, I be a wizard!' grinned Wilfred.

'Oh, er . . . right . . .' she replied, bemused.

Long-suffering librarian

Wilfred bowed again, and slipped out of sight behind a large bookcase. Spitting on his finger, he drew a pentacle on the wooden floor, and took his spell candle out of his rucksack and lit it. Then, stepping into the pentacle and clutching his Bag of Bees, he muttered the incantation for Ye Spectacular Summoning Charm and commanded any book containing magic (or rather 'magik', as he thought of it) to come to him.

There was an ear-splitting crack and a flash of light exploded around him, followed by a dazzling display of brightly coloured sparks. Wilfred screamed and ducked for his life, as literally hundreds of books flew off the shelves, across the library, and hurled towards him like a flock of demented pigeons. They thudded against the wall behind him and thumped onto the floor.

'Wild boars' widdle!' he cried, throwing his arms up to cover his head. (You'd be surprised to know just how many writers use the word 'magic' even if they're not writing a book about witches and wizards.)

Wilfred was speechless. He had performed Ye Spectacular Summoning Charm perfectly, on his first attempt, and with spectacular results! He'd summoned a veritable mountain of books! A thick pall of turquoise smoke wafted out from the book

shelves and across the library. 'Verily I be already becoming a mighty and powerful wizard,' he gasped proudly.

Sadly, of course, it wasn't true. Wilfred's skills *had* improved with practice, but as you've probably already rumbled, it was the dragon's claw talisman stashed within the Bag of Bees pouch that was giving him such enormous power.

'What on earth?' cried the long-suffering librarian, rushing over.

But Wilfred had seen the book he wanted in the middle of the heap. An impressively enormous tome bound in dark red leather, with gold lettering that said: *Ye Ancient Yet Complete Runic Record of Magik Charms and Enchantments*. Wincewart's grimoire! He'd recognise it anywhere.

(By the way, if you're wondering how Wincewart's ancient spell book ended up in the tiny library of Withering Wallop in the Wold, I can quickly tell you. Stashed in a box of other antique books, the grimoire was bequeathed to the library by Sir Edmund Kingsley Norton, the famous Victorian antiquarian and collector of curiosities. Goodness only knows how he got his hands on it. But one thing is certain – Ye Cheap Yet Cheerful Concealing

Charm was nowhere near as potent or effective as Wincewart had thought it was.)

Joyously grabbing his spell candle, Wilfred blew it out quickly. Then, ecstatically clutching the spell book under his arm, he clambered over the huge heap of books and belted for the door.

'Hey! You need a library ticket to borrow that!' yelled the librarian as he shot past her. 'And what about all this mess!'

But Wilfred had disappeared.

Wilfred consults the grimoire (briefly)

In the gutter of the High Street, in the middle of modern-day Withering Wallop in the Wold, Wilfred sat cross-legged, with Wincewart's grimoire open on his lap. He was scoffing his breakfast and impatiently flicking through the book, desperately trying to find the foretelling spell he'd used. But he couldn't, for the life of him, remember which one it was.

He sighed and gazed towards the ruins of the castle in front of him. The Midsummer Madness Wizarding and Witchcraft Festival was a hive of activity. *It be busier than a skep of bees in a flower meadow in high summer*, brooded Wilfred enviously.

He wondered how Bel and Jon were getting on, and he wished he were with them. He was surprised how much he missed Bel. He'd only known her a day or so, but it felt like he'd known her for ever.

He sighed sadly, remembering how much he'd upset her the previous evening.

Methinks I should go to the castle and find her, and tell her how sorry I be, he thought. *I will ask her to forgive me.* Because, he told himself, even if he could find the spell and work out how to send himself back, he couldn't go without seeing Bel and saying farewell. So, having finished his breakfast, and readily giving up the search, he shoved the spell book into the rucksack and strode off towards the castle, whistling cheerfully (and irritatingly tunelessly) and swinging his Bag of Bees as he went.

Chapter Twenty-Four

By the carbuncles of Cuthbert the Cautious!

Wincewart had woken a lot earlier than Wilfred. (About one thousand years, three hours and forty-five minutes or so earlier, to be precise. But that's irrelevant.) The main thing was he had woken in despair. For on this very day, in a matter of hours, he would be making a spectacle of himself at the merrymaking by *failing* to make a spectacle of himself by disappearing. The only thing that could save him was to get his dragon's claw talisman back from the future. And he had absolutely no idea how to do it.

He wasn't sure if he could be bothered to get up.

Bertram fluttered over and landed on his chest.

'Wincewart, I have been thinking . . .'

'And . . .?' said the wizard gloomily, lying flat on his back with his eyes closed.

'All be not lost.'

'Be it not?' queried Wincewart flatly, still with his eyes closed.

'No. Art thou or art thou not Wincewart the Withering, Castle Mage, Soothsaying Sage and the greatest wizard in all Wallop and the Wold?

'I be.'

'Then surely thou can find some other magnificent magikal marvel to perform? Something thou has not done before. And thou can always big it all up with a bold and bamboozling display of flashing lights, coloured smoke and showers of sparks,' the raven added cannily, with its head on one side.

The wizard's eyes shot open and he sat up, carelessly knocking the indignant familiar off his chest. 'By the carbuncles of Cuthbert the Cautious, thou art right!' cried Wincewart, throwing off his sheepskin cover and getting up.

Muttering feverishly and darkly into the remains

of his burnt beard, he grabbed his grimoire and trawled thought it. Eagerly scanning the charms and enchantments, the runic marks and magical symbols, he was determined to find something he could do *without* his talisman.

Something bold, something new, and above all, *flashy*.

After a few moments, he tapped an open page, harrumphed in triumph and turned to Bertram. 'I have the thing. It be high summer so I shall enchant the sky to snow!' he declared 'That will be flabbergasting!'

'Thou did that for Lady Wallop's birthday party,' Bertram reminded him.

Wincewart grunted crossly, then went back to his book and turned over a few more pages. 'Aha!' he cried excitedly. 'I shall turn a pumpkin into a pig! I am sure I could do that without the talisman. Well, maybe only a piglet – but it will be splendid!'

'But did thou not try that at Michaelmas?' croaked Bertram. 'They will surely remember. Thou does not often see a pumpkin sprout the legs, tail and snout of a pig and trot away, squealing.'

'Potent pentacles!' swore Wincewart, turning over more pages. 'Wait a moment! I have it! I shall make gold from straw! It be a remarkable feat! I have not done that before, I am sure of it.'

'Thou art right,' cawed the raven. 'Thou has never managed to do that at all – even *with* thy silver dragon's claw talisman. And let us face it, we would not be living here, in a gloomy cave if thou could!'

Wincewart sighed and went back to the spell book.

Ye Sensational Spindle and Scrying Glass Enchantment

Bertram the Beady thought for a while and then cawed, 'What be that one where a spindle be hidden in the castle and thou find it with the scrying glass?'

'Ye Sensational Spindle and Scrying Glass Enchantment,' replied Wincewart. 'But did I not perform that for the Lord Wallop and his nobles the night before his wedding?'

'Thou did. But methinks they were all far too drunk to remember it!' replied the raven.

'Thou art right!' cried Wincewart excitedly. 'We art saved!' (You will notice that, as usual, he failed to thank his familiar. Bertram didn't.)

'Thou art welcome,' Bertram croaked sarcastically.

But Wincewart was already sweeping up his scrying glass, grabbing his staff and heading off confidently – cheerfully, even – out into the sunshine and up the hill towards the castle.

'We must tell Lord Wallop of our small change in plan!' he called back over his shoulder.

Bertram fluttered over to travel the easy way, balancing on the wizard's shoulder, and he preened his glossy black feathers smugly on the way.

The Midsummer Merrymaking of Magik and Mages

The track to the castle was thronged with all manner of folk making their way to the merrymaking. From noble lords and ladies dressed in their finery on horseback, to barefoot snotty-nosed urchins running around in rags. You couldn't move for wizards and witches, travellers and traders, crofters and crafters, peasants and pages – the route was packed.

'Make way! Make way for Wincewart the Withering, Castle Mage, Soothsaying Sage and the greatest wizard in all Wallop in the Wold!' squawked Bertram loudly.

People hurriedly moved aside as Wincewart strode between them, clutching his scrying glass and cutting a path with his staff, his cloak billowing melodramatically as he passed.

Inside the castle walls the noise was deafening. Hundreds of people milled around laughing and yelling to each other, while stallholders hollered to be heard above the mayhem. Minstrels and musicians, jugglers, fire-eaters and stilt-walkers entertained the crowds while pick-pockets and cutpurses made the most of things behind their backs.

'This be impossible! How can I see the Lord Wallop amidst all this rabble?' cried Wincewart, so he sent Bertram the Beady to fly over the crowd and scout with his sharp eyes.

Chapter Twenty-Five

The Midsummer Madness Wizarding and
Witchcraft Festival

Funnily enough, at exactly the same moment but a thousand years away, Wincewart's apprentice was also struggling to push his way through a thick crowd of people milling around the castle grounds.

Frogs' gibbets! he thought. *How am I ever going to find Bel amongst all this lot?*

The size and spectacle of the modern day 'festival' staggered him. Over the centuries, as the mighty walls of the castle had crumbled, the merrymaking had expanded well beyond the fallen battlements.

As far as Wilf's eye could see there were throngs of people, many of them with their children and even their dogs. And there were more witches and wizards than you could shake a druid's staff at. He gave up looking for Bel and let himself be swept away by the sheer . . . well, *magik* of it all.

He wandered around dozens of stalls and tents, all selling a dazzling variety of magical goods, and stopping every now and then to watch some amazing display of magik or other. He saw a wizard cut a piece of rope into pieces and then magically *put it together again*! A young mage bent a metal spoon almost in half *without even touching it* and another one made an apple *float in mid-air*!

It was astonishing – the powers of the wizards in this strange new time seemed awesome.

It would be fair to say that Wilfred's belly always ruled his head. (Or, as Wincewart preferred to put it: Wilfred's empty belly always ruled his empty head). And his belly was definitely empty now. His mouth watered at the sight of, or to be more accurate, the tantalising *smell* of an enormous hog roast dripping hot fat and sizzling invitingly. His stomach grumbled loudly. (But then, all he'd had to eat for breakfast was a large sausage roll, two Danish pastries, a chocolate bar and packet of crisps – and that had been hours ago.) So now he was starving. He was also penniless.

'Haddocks' teeth!' he groaned.

He watched a couple of magicians doing some pretty simple magik. When they'd finished, much to Wilfred's surprise, people threw coins into a hat at their feet.

I could do that, I be sure I can, he thought. Well, he could if he had a hat. He wished Bel were with him – she'd have lent him her hat. Actually, he wished Bel were there, full stop. He didn't want her *only* for her hat. He was enjoying the merrymaking, but it would have been a lot more fun with her.

Wilfred the Wise is unwise

Undeterred by his lack of hat, he took an empty burger carton out of a rubbish bin. He could use that instead. There was a smear of ketchup on the inside, so he wiped it up with his finger and licked it. Then he took himself to an empty space and set up. Taking the chalk out of his cloak pocket, he drew a pentacle on the grass, and put the burger carton on the ground just outside it.

A few people gathered around him, intrigued. Then he stuffed the spell candle into the grass, and effortlessly enchanted it to light. There was a faint waft of turquoise smoke and an even fainter smattering of applause. Wilfred bowed modestly to his small audience, then took out the remains of Bel's pack of cards and stepped into the pentacle.

'Mine noble lords and ladies,' he cried, 'I be Wilfred the Wise, apprentice to the mighty wizard, Wincewart the Withering, and I will now perform some magik for thy delight.' Holding up a couple of Bel's cards for everyone to see, he added, 'Here be some cards. If thy keep watching I shall make them vanish, *before thy very eyes*!'

With great showmanship, and clutching his Bag of Bees charm, Wilfred chanted Ye Astonishing Disappearing Enchantment and commanded the cards to disappear. Which, much to his surprise, they did – instantly, and with a loud crack of thunder, a bolt of lightning, and a dazzling display of colourful sparks.

Wilf nearly jumped out of his skin.

It was mighty impressive. So he did it again. The

applause grew. So did the crowd, and so did Wilfred's confidence. He did it again, and again. Coins clinked into the cardboard carton. Pretty soon he had more than enough for lunch (although, truth to tell, he was beginning to run pretty low on cards.) But he was carried away by his success and didn't want to stop. So, turning to the crowd he boldly announced, 'Now I will astound thee still more! If thou pick an object, and hold it up, I shall make it disappear!'

Eagerly, the audience called out to him, holding out their belongings. So he casually disappeared a baseball cap, a pair of pink sunglasses and a half-eaten strawberry ice cream. The applause was thunderous, and by now he was surrounded by a very large and admiring crowd, and a very dense cloud of turquoise smoke.

Wilf was feeling mighty pleased with himself. But unlikely as it may seem, he still had absolutely no idea that it was actually Wincewart's talisman, stashed in his Bag of Bees, that was giving him such impressive power.

Chapter Twenty-Six

The Lady Wallop expects

Back in the middle of the Middle Ages, in the middle of the castle, in the middle of the day, it had not taken Bertram long to spot the huge, shaggy-red head and even bigger, shaggy-red beard (and the enormously girthed figure) of Lord Wallop. (As a matter of fact, Bertram's eyes were sharp enough to see the fleas hopping around in his hair too, but let's not go there.)

The lord of the castle was surrounded by his wealthy guests, and Bertram fluttered over his head like a hawk over a field mouse, signalling his position to Wincewart. Glancing down below him, the raven saw so much richness and finery he was sorely tempted to, well, drop a dropping or two. But with enormous self-restraint, he resisted.

'Wincewart!' bellowed Lord Wallop enthusiastically, as the wizard finally pushed his way through the crowd.

Bowing lightly, Wincewart asked if he could speak to him.

Wallop flung his arm flamboyantly around the wizard. 'Verily, my mighty mage! What can I do for thee on this, ye finest merrymaking day?' he roared. (The Lord Wallop had only one volume: deafening.)

'My lord, I have a surprise for thee,' announced the wizard.

Lord Wallop rubbed his hands together greedily. 'And what be that?'

'I will not be performing Ye Astonishing Disappearing Enchantment today,' continued Wincewart. 'Instead I will perform another far more marvellous mystical amusement to charm and delight, astonish and astound thee and thy most noble guests.' He paused for effect. 'I shall perform

Ye Sensational Spindle and Scrying Glass Enchantment!' he finished grandly.

'No, thou will not!' retorted Lord Wallop immediately. 'I have told everyone that thou will do Ye Astonishing Disappearing Enchantment. And so has mine lady wife.'

They both knew what that meant. Lord Wallop shot Wincewart a rather pained look, and the wizard gulped, nodded in understanding, and sloped off in despair.

It all goes horribly, horribly wrong for Wincewart

'Thou art doomed!' crowed Bertram in the wizard's ear for the second time that day.

Wincewart glared furiously at the raven, but his familiar was right.

Without his talisman, he Wincewart the Withering, the most powerful Wizard in all Wallop in the Wold, was doomed. Unless . . .

Frantically, Wincewart looked around the castle grounds at the multiple stalls and merchants selling all kinds of magical kit and caboodle.

'Bertram!' he cried feverishly. 'What if there be another dragon's claw talisman for sale here at the merrymaking? Why did I not think of that before?'

'Because thou art an idiot?' muttered the raven to himself.

'Quickly, thou must go and seek. And if thou find one, bring it to me.'

Bertram squawked indignantly as the wizard suddenly grabbed hold of him and flung him upwards into the air.

The wizard was confident that if such a talisman were to be found at the merrymaking, then Bertram the Beady with his sharp, penetrating eyes would find it.

There wasn't.

Wincewart's heart sank when Bertram returned without one. To add to his misery, it was exactly at that moment that Lord Wallop clambered up onto the stage and the crowd began to gather around expectantly for the grand finale.

'All be lost, master,' squawked Bertram into Wincewart's ear. 'I beg thee, let us flee before it be too late!

'Flee before thou make a fool of thyself before all these lords and ladies!

'Flee before thy reputation, and probably also thy cloak, are torn to tatters by the unruly rabble!

'Flee before the Lady Wallop, who as thou knows rules the castle with a rod of iron, reaches for that very rod of iron and ends your day, if not your life, extremely painfully!'

'Good plan!' cried Wincewart and, hitching up his cloak and robe, promptly tried to leg it unnoticed through the crowd. But in turning to run, he tripped over the small but impressively powerful figure of Lady Wallop.

'Wincewart!' she screeched in her high-pitched voice. 'Here thou art! Thou be needed on the stage.' And yanking him by the cloak, and leading him like a deerhound on a leash, the tiny woman dragged the mighty wizard to his fate.

Chapter Twenty-Seven

It all goes horribly, horribly wrong for Wilfred

On her way back from getting some cold drinks for her dad and herself, Bel noticed a sizable and cheering crowd. (Well, it would have been difficult not to, frankly.) She'd been keeping an eye out for Wilfred amongst the wall-to-wall wizards at the festival, hoping to see him. She had a funny feeling (well, a sinking feeling to be more accurate) that she'd just found him.

Pushing her way to the front of the audience, she arrived just in time to see Wilfred, with great panache and style, and to her utter astonishment, make three things vanish before her very eyes: a mobile phone, a posh flashy watch, and finally – and enormously unwisely – a small Chihuahua in a glittery pink collar.

The crowd gasped, but the owner of said Chihuahua promptly started screaming her head off. 'Where's my dog!' she screeched, leaping into the pentacle and grabbing Wilfred by his tunic and shaking him violently. 'What have you done with her?!'

Suddenly everything started going horribly, horribly wrong. Because although Wilfred had made lots of things disappear, very competently, and very impressively, he had no idea how to get them back again. It simply hadn't occurred to him that he would have to – until now. Which, frankly, was a tad too late.

Wilfred the Wise is an Idiot

Not surprisingly, the crowd quickly turned very angry, and virtually besieged him, demanding their things back, especially the owner of the small Chihuahua in the glittery pink collar.

'Where's my precious Pixie Pie?' she screamed, thwacking Wilfred with her bag. 'Call the police, someone!'

'Battered buttocks!' cried Wilfred, throwing his arms up to defend himself. Looking around desperately, he suddenly saw Bel. 'Help, my lady! HELP!'

To be honest, Bel had absolutely no idea what to do. She only knew she couldn't leave her mate to face the baying crowd alone. So, dropping her drinks, she courageously forced her way between Wilfred and the angry mob.

'Calm down!' she shouted authoritatively. 'CALM DOWN!' she bellowed again, her mind racing to think of what to say or do next. The crowd settled down and drew back, looking at her expectantly.

She should have been panic-stricken – there must have been about a hundred people staring at her. But, without any plan in her head, Bel's professionalism suddenly took over and she found herself saying, 'Ladies and gentlemen! This is all just part of the act! You don't seriously think Wilf – I mean, *Wilfred the Wise*,' she corrected herself, 'would make things disappear if he couldn't get them back again? Don't be ridiculous. I mean, honestly! The clue's in the name! Wilfred *the Wise*.'

The audience, re-assured and feeling a little foolish, settled down to enjoy the rest of the performance.

Turning to Wilfred, Bel muttered urgently, 'Stop mucking about. Bring everything back!'

'I can't!' he hissed.

'What? So let me get this straight,' Bel hissed back furiously. 'You made a mobile phone, a posh watch and a Chihuahua vanish into thin air – and you don't know how to get them back?'

Wilfred shook his head.

'You're an IDIOT!' she snapped.

Some of the crowd started laughing, thinking the banter between them was part of the act.

Wilf gave Bel his lopsided sheepish grin and anxiously ran his hand through his scruffy hair.

She rolled her eyes. 'Don't just stand there, think of something!'

Wilfred briefly thought about disappearing himself. But he didn't want to leave his friend alone to face the mob in case they turned angry again.

'My lady, I have it!' cried Wilf. 'I will make thee and me vanish too!'

'Are you crazy?' yelled Bel.

The audience roared with laughter.

'Wait – I *do* know what to do!' cried Bel. 'Do Ye Astonishing Disappearing Enchantment – but *backwards*!'

'Turnips' teeth! My lady, thou art brilliant!' gasped Wilfred. Immediately he tried to mentally reverse the incantation of the spell, then he had a stab at saying it out loud.

There was a mighty explosion, a bolt of lightning and a great cloud of colourful smoke.

Wilfred screamed and Bel jumped and swore out loud!

But the crowd, which was getting bigger by the moment, cheered and applauded thunderously.

So, unwisely, Wilfred tried again. But he only created more lightning and smoke, and a burst of worryingly hot red sparks.

'Wilf, STOP!' cried Bel. 'Do you actually know what you're doing?'

'No,' he admitted, 'But fear not, I have a book!'

Some of the audience were almost crying with laughter by now.

Frantically, Wilf wrenched Wincewart's grimoire out of the rucksack, and feverishly flicked through the pages. 'My lady, could thou just entertain these good peasants for a while?' he cried cheerfully.

'What?' replied Bel, horrified.

'I will not take long, I promise thee!'

'What, exactly, do you expect me to do?'

'My lady, thou art a talented magician! You could show them your skills!'

The crowd cheered their approval at the mention of more magic. For a brief, horrible moment Bel thought he was having a dig at her, because she could only do tricks rather than real magic. But then he gave her his lopsided sheepish grin again, and the look in his eyes was so honest she realised he wasn't.

'I can't,' she whispered at him urgently.

'Yes, thou can.'

'No, really, I can't.'

'No, really, thou can. Thou just think thou cannot. But I know that thou can. Trust me, I be a wizard!' he finished, winking at her encouragingly before urgently turning back to the spell book.

Nervously, Bel stood looking at the expectant mob while the expectant mob stood looking at her.

What if it all goes horribly wrong? And in front of all these people? she thought. *Oh, pull yourself together,* she told herself sternly. *The sky's not going to fall on your head. And, let's face it, you can't make the situation any worse!*

So she got her magic rings out of her rucksack and took a deep breath.

Chapter Twenty-Eight

Wincewart be in dire trouble

Meanwhile, back in ye olden times, Wincewart the Withering's reputation was hanging in the balance. He had no choice but to clamber onto the stage where Lord Wallop was grandly announcing the grand finale of the Midsummer Merrymaking of Magik and Mages. Wisely, or probably cowardly, Bertram the Beady left him to it and fluttered up to the castle battlements.

'Noble lords and ladies, travellers, guests and

peasants,' bellowed Lord Wallop. 'I give thee Wincewart the Withering, Castle Mage, Soothsaying Sage and the greatest wizard in all of Wallop in the Wold!'

The crowd cheered wildly. Lord Wallop put his hand up to silence them before carrying on.

'He will now perform a most stupendous magik spectacle for thy delight. Something that no mage or magician has ever done before.' He paused for effect. 'He shalt make himself vanish . . . and before thy very eyes!'

There were gasps from the audience, and Lord Wallop led the enthusiastic applause as he exited the stage, leaving Wincewart cringing in despair. Everyone gathered round expectantly, and it all went horribly, horribly quiet.

Wincewart did what any self-respecting wizard would do in such difficult circumstances, and grasped at straws. He did a few simple pieces of magik, amidst much smoke, colourful sparks and showmanship, and initially the crowd were entertained.

But firstly, they'd seen it all before, and secondly, they'd been promised so much more. Soon – painfully soon it seemed to Wincewart – the crowd and Lord Wallop himself began to demand the big finish. Impatient mutterings rippled through the crowd, together with infectious catcalls to 'Come on!' and 'Get on with it!'.

By now, Wincewart was in a full-blown, off-the-scale, heart-attack-inducing panic.

'Before I vanish,' he announced desperately, 'I will perform one more marvel of magik: Ye Sensational Spindle and the Scrying Glass Enchantment.'

'Thou has done that before!' cried one of the noble lords.

'And it was not that good then!' heckled another one.

Everyone roared with laughter.

Wincewart gave the mocking crowd a withering look and rose above the jeering.

Bravely, he took up a simple wooden spindle and his crystal ball. But he didn't need to look into the glass to see what the immediate future was going to bring.

It was a soggy cabbage and it knocked his hat off.

'How dare thee! I am the mighty Wincewart the Withering!' he thundered as a mouldy apple thwacked him in the face.

Cries of 'Boo!' and 'Pigswill!' and 'Get him off!' rose from the bored and cheated audience.

Heroically ignoring the barrage of rotten tomatoes and other assorted fruit and veg splattering onto his cloak, and ducking a very large and muddy leek, Wincewart took up the scrying glass and peered into its depths.

To his amazement, inky deep-blue smoke was swirling and filling the glass . . .

Chapter Twenty-Nine

Bel is B-Dazzling

'Right, so . . . well . . . ladies and gentlemen, I'm B-Dazzle, and this, er . . . as you know, is my talented colleague Wilfred the Wise, or Wilfred the *Un*Wise, as I like to call him!'

There was a burst of laughter.

'And while we give him a few moments to prepare . . . the . . . er, closing finale, I'll . . . er . . . I'll B-Dazzle you with some magic of my own.'

Crushing down the rising panic, Bel checked her hat was on at the right angle, and then held up the hoops. She glanced at Wilf behind her – he was still frantically searching through the spell book. She rolled her eyes and carried on.

'I take three, perfectly ordinary, solid metal hoops,' she continued, showing them to the crowd. Then she held two rings in one hand.

'Watch closely!' she commanded.

She tossed the pair of hoops up in the air, and caught them neatly in one hand, crying, 'Shazam!' When she held them out to show the crowd, the rings were linked together.

There was a small cheer and a round of applause from the crowd, then a loud

BANG!

and a huge

FLASH!

of lightning from Wilfred, and the entire crowd was enveloped in a cloud of turquoise smoke.

They cheered wildly.

Bel paused in her act. 'How's it going, Wilfred the *UnWise*?' she asked sarcastically.

'Not that well, my lady,' he replied, honestly but cheerfully. Everyone laughed and Bel decided to ignore the disaster in the background and just carry on. At least she knew *her* magic was going to work.

She rolled her eyes again, theatrically, and handed the two linked hoops to a man in the crowd. 'See if you can get them apart.' The man took a ring in each hand and pulled – but one was linked *inside* the other and there was no way he could pull them apart. He grinned and handed the hoops back to Bel.

'Ladies and gentlemen, now watch very closely!' commanded Bel and she started to rub the third hoop against the other rings – but before she had time to link them together with a triumphant 'Shazam' suddenly:

FLASH! KA-BOOM! WHOOOSH!

'Aaaargh!' yelped Wilfred, ducking a shower of tiny hot sparks and a bolt of lightning.

The crowd hooted and applauded madly.

'For crying out loud, Wilf! Try something else!' yelled Bel. 'Wait! I know! What about that summoning charm? Can't you use that?'

'Alas, I cannot summon something if I do not know where it is,' replied Wilfred. Then he slapped his forehead in frustration. 'Toads' teeth! Verily I do be a dolt and a dunderhead! I can use the *scrying glass* to look for them! And then when I find them I can summon them!'

'But if you find them you won't need to summon them,' said Bel witheringly, but logically.

'My lady, thou do not understand!' said Wilfred a little patronisingly.

'That's because you're talking nonsense,' replied Bel.

And the crowd burst out laughing again.

'I be not! Trust me, I be a wizard,' said Wilfred hotly.

'No you're not – you're an apprentice and a very poor one at that!' joked Bel.

Everyone roared with laughter.

Wilfred started digging round in his rucksack, looking for the crystal ball. Trying to ignore him, Bel carried on like a true professional to finish her magic hoop illusion.

'Where was I?' she joked. 'Oh, I know! I was finishing the amazing high magic art of melding metal!' And, rubbing the third hoop against the other rings

for the second time she cried 'Shazam!' once more.
Then with a flourish she held the three hoops out to
show they were all now linked together like a chain.

Overhearing someone say, 'She's very good, isn't
she!' she grinned broadly.

'How did I do that?' she challenged her audience
sassily. 'It's magic! I'm B-Dazzle – and you've been
B-Dazzled!'

The crowd roared their approval. Bel doffed her
hat and bowed.

Wilfred the Wise is awesome

Meanwhile, Wilfred had taken the scrying glass out
of his rucksack and was stepping into the pentacle
on the grass, ready to perform Ye Very Ancient
Seeing Spell.

But, peering into the depths of the glass ball, he
was astonished to see Wincewart – staring straight
back at him!

'WILFRED!' cried Wincewart.

'MASTER!' cried Wilfred and, clutching his Bag
of Bees (and of course the powerful talisman which
lay inside its pouch) he instantly decided on a daring
and truly brilliant change of plan.

Taking a breath, he confidently chanted the incantation for Ye Spectacular Summoning Charm and *commanded* Wincewart the Wizard to come to him.

There was an absolutely blinding flash of light, and an explosion of brilliantly coloured sparks like a full-on firework display, which crackled and burst, leaving a thick pall of turquoise smoke . . . and Wincewart the Withering, the most powerful wizard in all Wallop in the Wold . . . appeared out of thin air.

It was hard to know who was more astonished – the wizard, his apprentice, Bel, or the crowd.

It was a magnificent spectacle, which totally stunned and silenced everyone. You could have heard a spindle drop.

'Maybugs' belches,' breathed Bel. 'That was AWESOME!'

Wincewart and Wilfred stood frozen in shock, staring at each other like startled rabbits, and opening and shutting their mouths like gasping haddocks.

So with a good degree of quick thinking and confidence, not to mention a great deal of panache and style, Bel took control. Stepping in front of the two stunned wizards, she addressed the astounded audience.

'Ladies and gentlemen, I present Wincewart the Withering – the most powerful wizard in all eleventh century Withering Wallop in the Wold, and his apprentice, Wilfred the Wise, the most powerful wizard in all twenty-first century Withering Wallop in the Wold!'

The crowd all but exploded with enthusiastic cheering.

'And how did we do that?' she asked them sassily. 'It's magic!' I'm B-Dazzle and you have been *well and truly* B-Dazzled!' she announced triumphantly, then she took off her hat and bowed.

The applause was deafening.

Chapter Thirty

Another magnificent spectacle

Meanwhile, back in the eleventh century, and at the exact same moment in time (give or take a thousand years) there was a blinding flash of light and a dazzling display of brilliantly coloured sparks, which crackled and burst, leaving a thick pall of turquoise smoke, and Wincewart the Withering, the most powerful wizard in all Wallop in the Wold . . . disappeared into thin air!

It was a magnificent spectacle, which totally

stunned and silenced everyone. You could have heard a spindle drop.

In fact, they did. The wooden spindle the mighty wizard had been holding in his hand fell to the wooden stage with a clunk, as he hurtled forward into the future. (Wisely, unlike his apprentice, he had clung on firmly to his scrying glass with his other hand.)

The crowd simply couldn't believe their eyes! The Lady Wallop's mouth had dropped open, and lords and peasants alike exchanged incredulous looks. Bertram, meantime, had fainted with shock and fallen clean off the battlements.

'Weasels' warts!' cried Lord Wallop, instantly taking command and striding over to look all around and behind the stage. Then, with considerable difficulty, given his size, he bent down to look under the stage, and he even sent someone off to look in the beer tent. 'Wincewart?' he bellowed. 'WINCEWART! Wherefore art thou, Wincewart?'

And soon, as it became clear the mighty wizard was nowhere to be seen, and had in fact, *disappeared before their very eyes*, the crowd began to chant,

'WINCE-WART, WINCE-WART, WINCE-WART!' as they applauded and cheered the spectacular disappearance of Wincewart the Withering, Castle Mage, Soothsaying Sage and the greatest wizard in all Wallop in the Wold.

Chapter Thirty-One

Ye Potent Yet Foolproof Returning Enchantment

Despite having travelled a thousand years in the blink of an eye, and landing in an entirely new millennium, and being very elderly, Wincewart the Withering coped magnificently and managed to pull himself together.

Casually brushing bits of rotten vegetables from his cloak, he bowed to the crowd and then instantly, and wisely, demanded his talisman back from his apprentice. Wilfred dug the silver dragon's claw out of his Bag of Bees and handed it over gladly. Then, sheepishly, he explained the chaos he had caused.

Wincewart nodded sagely, and then, calmly but with an impressive display of colourful sparks, bolts of lightning, and billowing clouds of smoke (the ultimate in flashy showmanship), he reversed all of Wilfred's disappearing magik.

So the playing cards, the baseball cap, the pink sunglasses and the half-eaten strawberry ice cream re-appeared, followed by the mobile phone, the posh flashy watch, and finally Pixie Pie the Chihuahua – still in her glittery pink collar.

He was rewarded with instant and thunderous applause. Not to mention whoops and cheers, and even tears from the owner of the Chihuahua.

Wincewart immediately realised the impression his spectacular disappearance (and reappearance, *with Wilfred*) would make on the crowd and Lord Wallop back at the castle in his own time. His reputation would be assured, probably for the next thousand years or more.

So no sooner had Wilfred introduced Wincewart to Bel, his master announced they had to leave and *immediately*. There was not, he claimed, a moment to lose.

Hurriedly Wilfred gave Bel the library copy of Wincewart's grimoire. 'Can thou take that to the library for me?' he asked. 'Oh, and give this back to thy father,' he said, handing her the scrying glass. 'With mine most sincere thanks.'

'Sure,' nodded Bel, taking them.

Then he tried to give her back the rucksack with her playing cards and wind-up torch in.

But she told him to keep them. 'And you can have these too,' she added, handing him the metal rings.

'But my lady, thou art most generous,' said Wilfred, truly moved. Bowing deeply, he solemnly took off his Bag of Bees charm, and put it round her neck. 'That be for you, my lady, with mine sincere thanks. I was humbled to be thy apprentice, and thou has taught me much!' He grinned sheepishly, then added awkwardly, 'I be sorry I called thee a trickster and a fraud. Thou art *not* a trickster or a fraud. Thou art mighty skilled. Can thou forgive me?'

'Course! You don't have to apologise. Honest,' smiled Bel warmly. 'Trust me, I'm a magician!'

Wincewart was becoming increasingly impatient, anxious that the crowd back in his and Wilfred's own time might be dispersing, and the whole effect of their spectacular return would be lost. 'Wilfred, thou must say goodbye to the Lady Bel,' he urged. 'We must leave *now*!'

'I will never forget thee, I promise!' said Wilfred, suddenly throwing his arms round Bel and hugging her. 'Not in a thousand years!'

She hugged him back. 'Of course you won't! I'm B-Dazzle and you've been B-Dazzled!'

'And he art Wilfred the Wise and he has been most *un*wise,' said Wincewart the Withering, coming over and grasping his apprentice firmly by the arm. Then the elderly wizard bowed politely to Bel, and with his scrying glass in one hand and his apprentice in the other, he uttered the words of Ye Potent Yet Foolproof Returning Enchantment.

'Send those I name,
from whence they came:
Wincewart-the-Withering-Castle-Mage-
Soothsaying-Sage-and-the-greatest-wizard-in-all-
Wallop-in-the-Wold! And also his mangel-wurzel-
brained-dolt-of-an-apprentice-Wilfred.'

There was a dazzling burst of lightning, a shower of colourful sparks, and then they both disappeared, leaving nothing but a cloud of purple smoke.

The crowd applauded and cheered wildly and for a long time.

Bel, on the other hand, slipped quietly away. She'd only known Wilf for a couple of days or so, and was surprised how sad she was to see him go. She was going to miss his daft banter, his off-the-wall sense of humour, and his funny lopsided sheepish grin. Not to mention his amazing genuine knock-your-socks-off eleventh century magic!

It was a bit disappointing not to have managed to learn any real spells and enchantments from him, but at least Wilf had taught her she really did have a talent for magic.

She wondered if she'd ever see him again. She hoped so, because not only did she like him enormously, in her heart of hearts she knew she would never meet anyone like him again – not in a thousand years.

But then she remembered the Bag of Bees charm round her neck.

Maybe it really did have a little magic power in it, as well as a few bees? Clutching it cheerfully, she went off to jot down the incantations Wilf had taught her, before she forgot them, and give them a try. Maybe she would be able to snazz up her act with some real, live, genuine, knock-your-socks-off, eleventh century magik after all!

Chapter Thirty-Two

*The return of Wincewart the Withering with
Wilfred the Wise*

Back in the eleventh century castle courtyard, the
crowd were still chanting Wincewart's name and
stamping their feet. It wasn't long before their
loyalty was rewarded with a second dazzling display
– this time with purple smoke and sparks, as
Wincewart the Withering re-appeared on the stage
– and *with Wilfred the Wise at his side!*

The applause was instant and thunderous.

'Weasles' widdle and warthogs' wee!' muttered

Wilfred in surprise when he saw where they were.

'Truly, thou art the greatest wizard in all Wallop in the Wold,' bellowed Lord Wallop over the cheering crowd. He strode over to Wincewart and thumped him on the back. Wincewart coughed, but bowed graciously. 'Though thou had me worried for a while,' admitted Lord Wallop with a wink.

'Why? There was no need! Thou can trust me, I be a wizard!' replied Wincewart haughtily.

The crowed laughed and cheered.

Wincewart the Withering be impressed

Later that evening in the hermit cave, with a low midsummer sun setting outside, Wilfred happily tucked into a large, steaming helping of hedgehog stew and dumplings.

'Be there any more?' he asked hopefully, so Wincewart casually did Ye Easy Repeating Spell to refill the cauldron, and Wilfred dug in.

After supper, Wilfred begged to show off his new magik skills to his master. With a good deal of flashy style and showmanship, and copying Bel as best he could, he performed Ye Amazing Disappearing

Card Spell and made several of Bel's cards disappear. His master nodded his approval.

Truly, thought Wilf, *I must learn how to get the cards back before there art none left.*

Then using Ye Spectacular Summoning Charm he casually commanded his rucksack to fly into his hand (which it did on his first attempt, and without so much as a single accidental spark or wayward flicker of flame). Finally, taking out the wind-up torch, he modestly showed Wincewart and Bertram how he could command it to light and go out effortlessly.

It took a lot to impress Wincewart the Withering, the most powerful wizard in all of Wallop in the Wold (whichever century he was in). But nevertheless, the ancient wizard was amazed at his apprentice's performance.

Though nowhere near as amazed as he had been when Wilfred had so skilfully summoned him *into the future*! Clearly there was more to this dunderheaded, foolish, lumpen oaf of an apprentice than he had realised, he thought fondly. And he was mightily glad to have him back.

Wilfred the Wise (maybe)

'Clearly thou has learnt much whilst thou has been away,' Wincewart said, giving Wilfred a rare smile.

Wilf's eyes lit up and he bowed modestly. It was true, he had learned a lot from Bel – he just wished he had had more time to learn more of her clever tricks. Actually, he thought, he wished he had had more time with her, full stop. He was going to miss her, with her odd way of talking, and her sense of fun.

Being with her had been an adventure, full of surprises and laughter and with a lot of really nice food. He was missing her already, he realised. Hardly surprising, since she was the best friend he'd ever had – in a thousand years.

But, looking on the bright side, if he'd managed to travel to the twenty-first century when he was only an apprentice, then surely he'd be able to do it again when he was a powerful wizard! Which made him even more determined than ever to knuckle down and learn the mystical art and mysterious craft of magik.

'But has he learnt not to meddle with thy things?' cawed Bertram with his head on one side.

Wilfred nodded humbly.

'And not to meddle with magik thou does not understand?' added Wincewart gravely.

'I have, master,' nodded Wilfred solemnly.

Wincewart picked up Bel's metal hoops. 'What be these for?'

'They be magik rings,' replied Wilfred proudly. 'For a melding metal enchantment.' He bowed respectfully to Wincewart and continued humbly. 'Master, they be not for the likes of a mere apprentice like me. It be high magik and so I do give them to thee, as a token to say how I do be truly sorry for all the trouble I have caused thee.

Wincewart was touched. He really had missed Wilfred. And not just because of all the chores his apprentice did, which both he and Bertram had taken for granted. (And which, it won't surprise you to know, they would continue to take for granted.) The wizard had missed his apprentice's grubby face with its cheeky grin and his cheerful, if irritating, whistling. But he didn't want to admit that to himself, and definitely wasn't going to admit it to Wilfred.

Wincewart examined the magik rings carefully. He had never seen anything like them before, and had absolutely no idea what to do with them. But he wasn't going to admit that to Wilfred either, so he nodded wisely and said, 'These are indeed high magik and thou must not meddle with them.'

Wilfred promised he would not, then said proudly, 'Master, thou does not know, but thou art the subject of a *legend* in the future!'

'A *legend*?' scoffed Bertram rudely.

Wincewart glared at his familiar from under his bushy eyebrows.

'And they have named the village after thee! They do call it *Withering* Wallop in the Wold!'

Wincewart nodded his white-haired head wisely, tried to look modest, and tried even harder to ignore Bertram's utterly tactless and raucously cackling laughter.

'Does thou think that one day, if I study hard, then perchance I might become a powerful wizard, like thou art?' Wilfred asked his master tentatively.

'Perchance,' said Wincewart carefully, with his elbows on the table and tapping his fingertips together.

'And that I might truly be called "Wilfred the Wise"?'

'Ha! Not in a thousand years!' cawed Bertram mischievously.

But Wincewart smiled and said, 'Methinks thou might, if thou art wise enough to study hard and practise well.'

'Pigs' pimples!' cried his apprentice humbly, and a huge lopsided grin broke out across his grubby face. 'I will, my master. I will. Trust me, I be a wizard! Well, nearly!'

Acknowledgements

I am indebted to:

Sara O'Connor – for commissioning *Wilfred the (Un)Wise*, or rather, Clodwig the Clumsy, in the first place, and overseeing the early drafts;

Naomi Colthurst – for turning Clodwig into Wilfred and pushing me to find Bel;

Annie Beth and her pork-pie hat – for showing me where to find Bel;

Jenny Jacoby – for picking up more copyedits than you can shake a witch's broomstick at;

and

Mark Beech – whose anarchic wizardry in the

illustrations adds much hilarity to Withering Wallop in the Wold.

But above all, to Gaia Banks – my agent and talisman.

Cas Lester

Cas spent many years having a fabulous time, and a great deal of fun, working in children's television drama with CBBC. She developed and executive-produced lots of programmes including *Jackanory*, *Muddle Earth*, *The Magician of Samarkand*, *Big Kids* and *The Story of Tracy Beaker*.

Now Cas writes books for children, helps out at a primary school library (where she is Patron of Reading) and looks after her family full-time. She has four children, a daft dog called Bramble and she lives in Oxfordshire. Follow Cas on Twitter: @TheCasInTheHat